FOR THE *Love* OF A MAN

MELISSA COBB

Moral Statement

"When turning back is not an option."

Introduction

Do you want to know the most terrifying thing in the world? Let me tell you, it's when you have a shovel on your shoulder, a gun to your head and being told to dig your own grave.

Silently inaudibly mumbled, "Lord, I know you can change my situation as well as his heart. But if you don't, there will be some sad singing and flowers bringing for me."

When I spoke that in my mind lighting lit the sky. I glanced over my shoulder and saw that Marcus held the flashlight under his arm. He saw me peeping and gave me a shove in my back. I stumbled a few steps as he snarled with a hiss, "I can hear you. God's not listening to you. Quit talking in your head to HIM. Can't you see HE hasn't answered you yet?"

Those words made me tremble with terror of the unknown. But silly me here I am doing just that; slowly and non-passionately about to dig my own grave.

1

Marcus spoke as if he had a heart, "I loved you with everything I had but tonight love is dead."

We walked a few more paces as he said, "Stop here. This looks big enough."

There was a nice size hole. It appeared to be about ten feet wide and four feet deep already. He looked at me staring and spoke, "Get in that hole and dig."

As I stared at him, he did that look. I put the shovel down and I hopped in the hole. He kicked the shovel at me, and it fell onto the ground by me. It would not take me long to dig but if I go slowly, it will. Dropping my head I wondered *how I ever loved such a man.* I picked up the shovel and decided to take my time. I put the end of the shovel on the ground and spoke sorrowfully. I really hoped he would pity me when I said, "The ground is too hard Marcus. I can't dig."

As if Mother Nature was playing a trick on me, thunder roared, and it began to rain. He glanced up towards the sky and laughed a laugh out of this world. He stared down at me with a smile as he said, "Guess your God hears you after all. Now dig!"

I whimpered like never before as the hard end of the shovel came into contact with Mother Earth. How could I still believe in an escape if I am digging into the now soft ground for a bed? From out of nowhere he spoke nicely but tauntingly, "I don't want to kill you but it's my destiny to kill you. If I don't do it, I won't be able to live with myself. I have been through so much with you.

At least in my mind, it would not seem right if I DIDN'T DO IT!

As the love of my life said that unloved testimony to me my soul closed, and my hands would not cooperate. I cried inside my eyes. I did not feel the presence of God but knew I had to quote in my mind that nothing happens to HIS chosen vessels without HIM knowing. For some reason enough I didn't feel happy about the fate of knowing I am to die at the hands of my husband, my lover, my abuser. Interrupting my mind were the words, "More digging, less thinking! I'm getting too anxious to pull this trigger multiple times in you" Marcus said with anger.

I became an on and off switch as I shut down my thinking and cried. Even the rain stopped to hear my thoughts as I began to think back. When I was a child, I thought about *how I used to fantasize about love, happiness, and family.*

I remembered how I played with the most sought-after dolls of my time, which were Barbie and Ken. I saw how my parents interacted; therefore, I would make them kiss when I moved Ken to and from the house. I would have Barbie in the kitchen cooking for Ken and she would serve him his dinner; all of this was to prepare me in the fantasy world of how to be a wife.

From my manners, my way of dress and how I interact was teaching me how to be that woman when I become her. But my real-life Barbie came from my mom.

She was the prime example of the Barbie I wished to imitate. She was beautiful when the need be, a happy servant to my father and stern mother to my brother, Samuel and I if the time came. If she and my dad disagreed, I never knew it. They kept all that away from us because their job was to make us happy, and they did.

To me, my parents were the model that I wanted my marriage after; therefore, I did all I could to make sure it would happen. When I met Marcus, I thought I found what I was looking for. I was at an exit program for teachers that have obtained their master's in education when I saw him. He was the guest speaker and all the graduating girls thought he was so fine to be as old as he was.

I tried not to notice how he was medium, with arms that could carry you away. I cannot forget the dark chocolatey skin that was hand. painted by God Himself. His clean-cut black and white hair was impossible not to notice, but when he spoke, that hypnotizing voice, would make you do whatever he wanted But it is up close that you could see his tempting smile and those alluring eyes that a man could ever have. Those attributes alone, would do something to your lower body part. It is here, I could understand why they all would throw themselves in his presence. When he came up to me, I was at once drawn to him, just like the rest.

We females are not complete until we have that one male in our lives that we will go over and beyond for. However, he would be the one that put butterflies in your stomach just by his touch. He would be the one that made you smile when no one else could. Just his name alone would brighten any dreary day. He would be your all in all and for him you would give the world too; just being in his presence, made you aware that you were a woman in need of a man.

After meeting back up a year later, we dated and got married. You talk about happy; I was her. He did everything in his power to be a stable provider and a caring husband. Whenever I was down, he encouraged me and when I needed understanding we prayed and sought God for HIS way. It was perfect because my husband was the man of the very dream I dreamed when I was a mere child.

We started talking about having a family and how family structure is especially important to us. I devoted more time to God and my husband. Marcus had a reversal vasectomy and like other couples, I didn't become pregnant right away. When I did, after two months the baby died in the womb right in front of us.

The look on his face was priceless as his emotions strolled outward. My husband tried to be strong for me, but he cried harder than I did.

The sight of seeing the heart not beating hurt me and traumatized Marcus deeply. He threw himself in his work and nothing I did soothed him. He was distant and his entire persona changed. He turned his back on me as if it were my fault. All the ingredients of a disastrous marriage were in play as he began yelling at me, but I made a choice to stay. I began seeing a Christian marriage counselor.

She recommended that I tough it out and let God do it. She also told me to continue to live my life before him as a wife would.

How do you hang in there and wait on God? How do you live a life before a man, that did not see you. I struggled with those questions because they confused me. I thought I was already waiting on God to do it. I know my Lord has all the answers, but my prayers were not being answered. This man I swore to love in front of all I knew constantly criticized me and I did not know why. However, I continued to pray for him, me, and this marriage but no avail was in sight.

In doing so I called myself letting God have it but the quieter I was the angrier my husband became. But when I would question him about the anger, the depression and pain, he would turn into someone I did not know and did not want to know anymore. I thought I had had, enough especially the day he punched me repeatedly in my face. Personally, he must have seen how beating up on me made him feel better; so, an evil alteration must have been activated. He would snatch me up, smile deceitfully and continue to do unkind things to me.

This is the first time outside my youth that I was ever hit or talked to in such an offensive style. Sometimes I would beg for my life just for him to leave me alone. Most of the time it would work and most of the time it wouldn't. When it did work, he had gotten tired of hearing me begging him to stop then and only then he let me go and walk off like nothing happen.

I would lay there battered and afraid for my life. The more agitated he got the more his abuse would be. The worse were the psychological ones. He would play with my mind by making a giant out of a mole hill. I could sit on the edge of the bed, and he would kick me off or put his fist mightily in my back; all because he could. Sometimes I did not see him and even if I wanted to; I couldn't or was too scorned. My once thriving life became one of shame, horror, and doubt.

I felt trapped. I know I love him, and he loves me, but this way of living is neither right

*nor just. I had no one to talk to. He divided
everyone from me and when people were around,
I would not speak much, in fear that I would give
way, to his true nature. Factual, I didn't want
anyone to see me. I didn't think they would
believe what I had to say. I do not even believe all
these things are happening to me. It is like being
under a spell that made you terrified to wake up.*

*Who would think it was my fault if all I ever
done was to please him? Who would think that I
brought this on myself when I could not make him
happy anymore or be happy? Me, that is who
because I began to blame myself. I was no
longer jolly, and neither was he; all I wanted to
do was stay out his way and out of everyone's
sight. I wanted to be unknown, and he did that.*

*Marcus took everything from me, mainly my
identity. He changed my name to Child because
he said I didn't deserve to be called by my real
name. He said Sarah is a name I had to re-earn
all over again and in time I could be her again. I
didn't inquiry him about it. I just took it and ran
with it.* Just like thunder in a storm brewing, I

heard "Quit thinking and dig faster before I shoot you and let the birds pick you to pieces."

The rain had stop. I stammered back loudly with passion, "I could have killed you, but I didn't!"

To mock me, he used a nursery rhyme, "Could of, would of, should of but you didn't. You didn't do it. You couldn't do it and I'm not going to keep telling you to shut up and dig."

My thoughts closed, and I dug faster in a circle. He could not stop me from praying and digging. Under no circumstances did I let up. I know he can't do anything to me if it is not my time. It was hour after hour as the blade end hit the earth to swing dirt over my shoulder to the top of the ground. Marcus shouted, "Stop digging. You have dug deep enough."

Just like that. I made the hole deeper than I imagined, which allowed me to stand in a grave that was eye level to the ground. As Marcus stood at the edge of the grave, he hovered over me, and spoke casually, "You know I never thought I would see the day, I outlive my young beautiful wife. If I hadn't heard the sticks, you would be happier now."

His eyes were on me like that of disgust as my eyes never lost sight of him. I didn't know what to think. Giving me that award winning smile, he got on his knees and waved for me to come even closer. I didn't want too but I knew if I didn't, he would shoot me quicker. Being careful, I eased over to him. He pointed the gun towards me and…………………

The Beginning

Chapter 1

Today is Saturday evening and I thought my husband would have come home last night but he didn't. I checked my cell and saw the texted stating that he loves me and that was it. Soon as I sat in front of the mirror, I saw Marcus's reflection. A smile lit my gloom face. I jerked around as he said, "Your brother is here, my love, on the front porch."

I raced to my feet. He surprised me as I nearly jumped out my skin. I thought he was gone but here he is in person. For the last day or so I have been awaiting the arrival of my spouse and now, he is here. I didn't care to ask questions as to when his flight made it back for, I didn't care. He was home and I am thrilled. In haste, we kissed like there was no tomorrow. Marcus had been gone for a little over two weeks while I was here at home, teaching Calculus to promising high school graduates. Pulling back, he said, "This can wait, love."

Begging like a sleepy person wanting more time to sleep I stated, "No give me five more minutes."

He laughed and spoke teasingly, "I will give you much more when your brother leaves."

My husband leaned over and gave me an exceptionally light kiss as he left out the room. I checked my makeup and one-piece dress while I stood in the mirror. I can't concentrate on talking to my brother because husband has placed sex on my brain. I smiled and walked to the porch where my brother Sam was sitting. It just strikes me as odd that he wanted to see me. Like many times beforehand, my words were that of joy, "Hey Sam how you are doing?"

"I'm good sis, how about you.'

"Won't complain but what brings you here?"

"I had a dream about you and had to see if you were ok."

He stunned me when he said a dream. Marcus looked at me and spoke, "It's quite naturally to dream about those you hold dear to you, Sam."

"You right" I added.

"This one stood up like no other. You were in a small dark room crying. You wouldn't look at me or say anything; you just kept crying."

"Where was I in this dream?" Marcus asked.

"I don't know where you were, but Sarah appeared frightened and alone."

"Sam, I can assure you, your sister isn't frightened or alone."

Wrapping his arms around me, he snuggled me closer to him. I inhaled the very scent of his clothing and that was a turn on. Deciding to move back, I got up and Marcus asked, "Where you are going, love?"

"To fix us a drink."

He stared at me and Samuel said, "I'm not thirsty."

"He's not thirsty. I'm not either but you can fix you a drink if you want."

15

I happily sat back down as Samuel spoke, "Let me finish telling you what I dreamed about."

Showing a smile, I shrugged my shoulders as Samuel said, "You were terrified, and I don't know what was wrong. You would never say what the matter was. I am here to tell you that I love you and if you need me, I am here for you."

Before I could reply, Marcus modestly proclaimed, "That is so thoughtful of him, isn't it honey?"

I smiled and lay my head on my husband's shoulder to agree.

Sitting up on the edge of his rocker Samuel said, "Well sis you know I am not a firm believer in dreams, but this was so real. Why else would I be over here?"

"Sam to see Marcus of course."

He and I laughed because I was being honest. Sam said, "True but I added you today because of the dream."

"Now I feel grateful."

My brother and I laughed some more. Marcus said, "Excuse me for a minute. I'll be right back."

Soon as he left us alone, Samuel asked "Would you tell me if something was really wrong? I mean lately I have been having a bad feeling, and I can't shake it."

Startled that he would ask me this was unusual. I replied, "I don't think there's nothing to tell. Just keep me in prayer if anything because we all need that."

Looking at the door and speaking ever so soft he spoke, "You right and I will but Sarah, you can tell me what it is if you need too."

All I could say was "Samuel" as I sat back on the swing. Marcus opened the screen door. He looked at me and asked, "Did I interrupt your conversation?"

Samuel gave him one of his "crazy looks" and we all laughed.

"Let me go. I must pick up some lumber to finish my fence."

"You need some help?" Marcus asked.

"No. I can manage today but I will check back later."

"Okay."

My brother gave me a hug. I didn't want to see him leave but I have a personal agenda that requires him to be gone. I hugged him tightly.

After breaking up the embracing, Samuel was leaving as I waved by from the porch. I went in the living room to wait. Marcus eased through the door. Hearing a sound, I saw he had locked it. Walking towards me with caution, he stood before me smiling and proclaiming, "I'm ready to make love to you now, Mrs. Grady."

Thinking of having my husband made me grin even more. Since he was no longer the principal, he took on the job of doing workshops and assessments for people in education. That job is six days a week job and most of the time it's out of town. He and I don't get to be together

18

a lot, but we manage. Honestly, Marcus is brilliant and hard working.

However, when he isn't teaching teachers how to teach their classrooms, he would be all over the place from South Haven to Pascagoula, as well as commuting from Memphis to Florida. I don't like his assessment job, but it pays very well and any time I can travel with him, I do. We tend to think of those getaways as mini vacations.

Lifting his hands to touch my cheek, I forgot all about what I was thinking. Removing his dress shirt, my fingers interlocked in the curly hair upon his ripen chest. Placing my palm onto his skin caused his nerves to run because I could feel the trembling under his skin. Kissing with ease, I muffled my face into his chest and teased him mightily. Soft moans escaped his lips as my fingers fumbled with his pants button.

Marcus laughed as he helped me. He said, "I'm too anxious to have you, my love."

"Likewise," he said. My breathing became raspy with anticipation and the thrill of making love in the living room. He tore off the one-piece dress and buttons flew everywhere. I giggled a little. Marcus said,

"Don't worry I can buy you another one."

As he spoke those words, he pulled me near to kiss me fervently all about my neck. Each kiss upon my flesh was like a hot brand on the skin.

The way he used his tongue to cool the fiery kisses was driving me wild. I, in return, returned the kisses with much hunger as possible. This man was causing my senses to be overloaded as his arms tighten upon me. Marcus was not letting me go and neither was I want to be released from his hold.

It was more inviting than ever. The way we carried on, there was no way we were making it to our bed chambers. I didn't care where he took me as long as he was having his way with me. Marcus felt the same for he briefly stared down at me. My eyes were screaming more as my body yarned for him. Gently, as if I would break, my husband laid me upon the couch and touched me with his massive hands.

He knows I am yelling more but this torture only increases my wanting for him. Seeing that I was not in the mood for patience he toiled and massaged each breast with light contact of lips and hands. My dear was enjoying this as much as I was, but I have needed him; therefore, I can do without the foreplay.

Sensing the urgency in my body I opened my legs. The moment he entered me was powerful and incredible. Marcus was taking his time to please me on a more intimate level. With each demanding thrust my husband was causing my legs to wiggle and my voice shouted his name. He could only moan as I stared into his wonderful face.

The orgasm was unique as we climaxed together. Still posted between my legs, he hovered over me smiling and shaking. Not wanting to let him go, he moved anyway to lie beside me. As he placed his arms around me, I began to sleep soundly. It has been a while since we made love on this magnitude. The way my husband took my body was emotional and spellbinding. It wasn't until the next morning that

21

we awoke, hungry and I sexually excited as I placed my hands on him with a familiar touch of sex. He said, "I can't do crap until I get a bite to eat."

Sounding preppy, I exploded my words, "That just means I must feed you, make love to you, feed you again, bathe, make love, feed you, make love, bathe."

Laughing he replied, "Slow down love. I don't have any more workshops to do for the rest of the week. But while you are at work I must plan for the upcoming sessions and seminars on Child Abuse, how to make math easy, Child Neglect, Making learning family fun and Classrooms Set-ups."

"Those preparations are not going to last all night, I assumed?"

Kissing me on my bare shoulder, he replied "No because my nights will be spent with the woman I love."

Kissing him back I stated, "And this woman loves you just as much."

Pulling back some he said, "Don't worry I won't be so fast but seeing you and smelling you made me anxious."

"I didn't realize you weren't going slowly because I was in as much need of you as you were of me."

Marcus got off the couch and grabbed me by the hand. Softly he spoke, "Come on let's go bathe and go out for breakfast."

Like the many school aged girls I have seen go behind a boy, I was like that with my husband as we went to our bedroom to the shower. He went in first while I got my clothes out. Soon as he finished, I went in behind him. When I came out, he was ready and looking as handsome as ever. I dried off and put on my clothes.

Marcus placed his arms around me and smelled my hair. He has always done that, and I have always loved him doing that. I spoke with a taunt, "I thought we were going out?"

"We are beautiful."

Inching my body more on him, I acknowledged "If you don't release me, we won't be going anywhere Mr. Grady for another hour or so."

He gave me one last kiss before letting me go. I went out the kitchen door first as he locked the door. I was already sitting in the car as he got in. Locking down his seat belt, he turned the car on, backed out and asked, "What you have the taste for?"

"It is eleven a. m. How about some Subway? I could use chicken teriyaki with extra olives and banana peppers."

"Sounds like you've wanted this for a while."

"I haven't eaten this since you left."

"How has things been at work?"

"Hectic. It is the first nine weeks, and the football players are not doing so well."

"All of them?"

"No just two of the main ones. They are smart and can do their work; they just choose not to do it. I have personally contacted their parents and told their coach of their classroom performance and nothing drastic has happened."

"What you going to do?"

"They have to pass this upcoming test if they want to finish the rest of the season playing and not on the bench."

"You are doing right Sarah. Football is a privilege, and they must score in the classroom before they can score on a field."

Marcus went to the drive through window and ordered our food. My mouth became watery for the food as he handed it to me. He drove off and asked, "You want to go to the park, since we missed service this

morning?"

"Yeah, we can do that and go to evening service."

We went to the park close by the house. We usually get out but today we didn't because people had dogs everywhere. The both of us stayed inside the car and ate our food. It was wonderful as I was getting full. Soon as we finished, Marcus got out and lit a cigarette. I was in awe.

He finished and got back in, but I didn't smell the usual scent. I had stated, "I thought you quit."

"I did."

"Then why you call lighting up?"

"This job is stressful and if I don't smoke, I will become a drunk," Marcus said to make a funny.

Giving into the play I mocked, "I would rather you did neither but if I had to pick a poison for you, I would pick drinking because smoking kills."

Laughing he replied, "So does getting in an airplane or driving into oncoming traffic."

"Funny but I am serious."

"I know but look at this cigarette."

He handed it to me, and it was one of those electronic cigarettes that looks real and even smoke like a real one. I questioned, "You trying to quit a habit you haven't done since we been together?"

"The other day I got so stressed that I almost bought a pack to smoke. Then I remembered about not wanting to destroy the body God gave me, so I bought that instead."

"In time you will be finished with that too but if your job is getting to you quit."

"I love what I do."

To question him I asked, "More than your health?"

"No but."

"But what?"

"I want to do diverse things but don't know what? Education is all I have ever done."

"You can limit the sessions you do."

Sounding a little down he said, "That won't help because I love doing as many as those as I can. I love to impart helpful information into the minds of inspiring teachers or old hands."

"You can take a break."

"I thought about that but what would I do in the meantime?"

As he questioned me, I thought about it, and *nothing came to mind*. Then I thought more, He is a lot older than I am, but age is just a number even if he is fifty-five. He has four children by his first wife with their ages ranging from thirty-three-year-old Katie and her four girls, thirty-one-year-old Tonya and her two girls, twenty-nine-year-old Marianne and her one boy and twenty-seven-year-old Elizabeth with no children. They are all girls, and they don't really talk to me and me them.

Their mom Sharon was ok with me at first, but she saw how he was doing a lot of things for me and taking me places that he never took her. Jealousy set in and now she has smart remarks when she talks to him about their seven grandchildren.

Once she said that he doesn't really love me and so on. It took a lot out of me, not to stoop to her level but now she does not bother me at all. Marcus gave me a light push, "Sarah you, ok?"

"I was just thinking. That's all."

"You ready?"

"Yeah."

He drove back home. The further he went through traffic I asked, "What about a career change?"

"Like?"

"You like education go back to doing that but at an elementary school."

"I thought about it, but I hadn't been stable in a classroom in years."

"You can be a youth counselor."

"That might be a clever idea I could do but the money isn't as sweet as what I am doing now."

"You being happy on your job is the upmost important than how much money one provides."

"How about if I retire and fish?"

"If that is what you want to do?"

Glancing towards me with those beautiful brown eyes and that hypnotizing voice, he declared "That's why I love you, Sarah. You don't crowd me, and you stick behind any idea I may have."

"That's what a woman does who loves her husband."

Marcus gave me a grin as we pulled up. I have made it. A big house, a wonderful job, a man that loves me and I'm well to do. I can eat what I want, and I can buy almost what I want. My marriage has been wonderful out of the short time we been married, which includes dating. We get along well as a couple and as friends. My husband makes me laugh when I don't want too, and he keeps me on my toes. It is never a dull moment with him and being with him gives me so much joy. Marcus

tapped my leg and asked as he drove closer to home, "What are you thinking about now?"

"I was thinking about how much joy you give me and how blessed I am to have you."

"I feel the same way."

He turned into our driveway. I stated, "Let's get out and rest up before service this evening."

Chapter 2

We got out of the car and went inside. Once inside we changed into some comfortable clothes. Marcus put on pajamas and a movie for us to watch as we snuggled up on the same couch, we made love on. After two hours, we ate a small snack and got ready for service. Parts of me were dreading church because his ex-wife and children still attend this church. They are respectful when they are not acting like I have a disease. Truth be known; their dad came after me. He and his ex-wife Sharon was not together before I came in the picture.

It is because I am younger than all of them, but they will be all right. We got ready for church and left. Arriving at church I felt better. I did not see his daughter's vehicles or Sharon's. That gave me semi-home. Soon as the pastor began to pray, they all came in and my happiness plundered. Marcus smiled at the sight of his children and grandchildren. I gave a hint of cheerfulness but not much. Turning back around, I began to listen to the pastor speak on "Holiness without can't no man see God."

He was saying that you must be holy to see God. Sin and God can't live in the same room. The pastor went on to say how you must have the Spirit of God in you and for you to worship HIM you must do it in Spirit and in truth. Everything the preacher was saying was on time and good to my ears. I wish he would have taught on honor thy parents. Even if I am not their birth parent, I am still their parent. I haven't wronged any of them and I am tired of faking. Marcus doesn't know how they do me and if we disagree it is because of them.

To avoid it all I speak and go on with my business. I don't give them time to lie on me as they have done in the past. Those girls are his world, and he believes them. I could tell him how they are acting towards me, and he would say it's a female thing or I misunderstood their actions or words. There is no way you can confuse words; I don't like you or daddy's new baby girl. Even the rolling of eyes or the silly laughs when I am near them.

Sometimes I must admit, when they want a favor, I tell him no, we have made plans, or I will pout. He will give in to what I want, and they get mad. It's like a tug of war and it should not be so. Turning my head, to face the pastor, his oldest daughter turned her nose up at me. I smiled and

placed my head on her dad's shoulder for the fun of it. Twisting my head some, I saw her take in a deep sigh. Marcus kissed the top of my head.

I lifted my head up and listened on. Moments later, it was time to take up the offering and tithes. I put my money in the envelope and so did Marcus. One thing I have learned and that is he pays his money faithfully and on time. All these things I am witnessing are new because I came out of a church where the preacher didn't speak against sin nor did any prophesying.

The pastor asked everyone to line up for prayer. I got behind Marcus and I heard as the pastor told him that he is about to do a complete change and how he must be careful. My first thought was how we were just talking about that. He prayed for my husband. When Marcus sat back down, he asked me to lift my hands. He said,

"I hear your faith is being tested and soon enough you will know where you stand in the

Lord."

Puzzled was the look on my face. I received the prayer as his daughter Marianne stared at me. Marcus stood up to let me in. I did not get a chance to sit at all because the Pastor asked us to remain standing for

the closing of service. We all recited the creed and had to hug a neighbor for dismissal. His daughters all came to him as I was talking to other church members. Out the corner of my eye I saw Sharon coming. I tried to get away, but it was too late. She stood in my way and asked, "Where's my hug Sarah bug?"

Being cautious I gave her a hug. She held onto me to say, "Come see me tomorrow when you get off from work."

Pulling back, I replied through a tighten mouth, "I will try."

"Please I insist."

I couldn't curse her out, especially in church so I spoke as nicely as possible, "If I don't forget or have time."

Cunningly she replied, "Thank you Sarah bug."

As she walked off, I saw one of my co-workers. I didn't know Mr. Trey Goss was at service visiting. He is a nice guy and has not ever said words or gestures out the way to me. I've encouraged him in the past when he loved Marcus's daughter Elisabeth, other than that friend. Marcus walked over to me as Mr. Goss was coming. They met up and chatted away on the current topics and the war on underfunded schools. I was just listening to them and was ready to go home. I nod my head and Marcus saw it as he spoke, "It was nice talking to you, but I am sure Mrs. Grady is ready. You ready love?"

Having a tired tone I replied, "I am. It has been a long day for me, and I can't wait to get some rest."

"I understand, Mrs. Grady. Today has been a long one for me as well," Mr. Goss spoke with a smile.

"Mr. Goss we will catch up and chat more; when it's just us men. You know how women folk can be."

They laughed as Marcus and I both said, "Bye Mr. Goss."

"Goodbye, Mr. and Mrs. Grady."

We walked a few feet away and Marcus mumbled, "He wants you, doesn't he?"

Under my breath I retorted highly above a whisper, "We've had this conversation before, remember?"

Retorting back were the words, "We might have but you are my wife."

"I know that love," I spoke in confidence.

"You know he use to date Elisabeth, but broke it off with her when you started working at the school."

"I'm sure I had nothing to do with that. I had no idea they even dated until I started seeing you and he told me."

"I know you say the same thing."

Smiling I stated with assurance, "The truth never changes."

Forgetting about our conversation he saw his daughter and asked normally, "Have you spoken to the girls yet?"

If I make up a lie it'll be an argument. To cut down any heartless discussions I stated, "They were talking to you earlier but come over with me."

He walks with me as we went outside to see the girls talking with their mother. We made our way towards them and slowly they peeled off one by one.

The grandchildren laughed as they talked to their pawpaw, while I watched idly before speaking to the grandchildren. After that I went to the car. Moments later he got in on the passenger side and asked cheerily,

"You like the service this evening?"

"I did very much. How about you?"

"I did also. The word was on time, but I will be better once I get to lie beside you."

I smiled. Seconds later, he was quiet before asking, "What Sharon say to you?"

That caught me off guard for I had forgotten all about her and what she said.

Loudly I stated, "Oh! She asked me to come by her house when I get off from work."

"I know you going right?"

With a question in my tone, I asked slowly, "Should I?"

"I think it would be good if you went. The girls will get a chance to see you and you all can have great conversations. It would be wonderful for you all to squash this power trip."

Sounding unsurely, I replied, "I don't think that will ever happen in this life."

"Why not? They try to be friendly towards you, but you act like they are less than you."

I nearly jerked the wheel when he said that to me. I spoke, as nicely as ever, "I do try to be civil to them, but they don't want that. They want confrontations, drama and so forth. They want things of this nature, and I don't plan to give it to them."

He was straight forth when he spoke, "I think you are being ridiculous about it and making something out of nothing. My daughters adore you, they have so much as told me that themselves."

"They must have been talking about each other because they can't stand me, and they are only hospitable because you are near but let you leave out. Their antlers come up and anger spits out their mouths."

"You don't know what you are saying. My daughters have no reason to lie to me about you."

"Well, they are lying to you about how they feel about me now."

40

We both were quiet as I ask, "Can we not talk about them? I don't want our conversations to be about them. Just the very mention of your children brings contentions to our marriage, and I don't want that. You just got back, and I want to be lovable."

Marcus was still quiet, and I didn't like that. I reached over to touch him, and he moved his hands. I politely put my right hand back on the wheel to drive. The rest of the ride home, he was solemn. He has

never gotten like this before, and it was unusual to see him like this. Making up my mind to remain quiet I did so. He would not even look at me. All the times we disagree it is because of his children.

He thinks he has angels, but I know better. I can't seem to make him see that. Maybe it's because I don't have children, and my parents treated my brother, and I like gold. That makes no difference because we weren't cunning or showing a good side evil side; on the other hand, my stepdaughters are. Placing the car in park,

Marcus got out and closed the door behind him. At this point he has not spoken to me. I gradually got out and went inside. Locking the kitchen door, I went to our bedroom. He was changing as I asked, "Are you okay?"

"I'm fine thank you," he spoke in a snapping tone without even looking at me.

His attitude was bitter and mean. Trying to make the situation better I stated, "I can have a dinner here and invite your children, kind of like a peace offering dinner. We dated for a year before we got married when you and Sharon have been divorced for the same amount of time. They may blame me for the breakup."

"How is that when Sharon and I were separated when I met you?"

"Yeah, but the entire time we dated you were still married to their mother legally just separated. Once your divorce became final, we married shortly thereafter."

"I'm already stressed and don't need any of this today. With that being said, can you shut the hell up please and that is putting it nicely?"

That threw me completely. Marcus has never said any rude language at any time and he is saying that to me was a shocker. He saw my face and said, "Just drop it and leave me alone."

With my nose turned up I spoke conceitedly, "Consider it dropped."

He rapidly stopped putting on his night clothes to say, "Didn't I tell you to shut up? I've asked you nicely and I will not ask you again."

Defensively I spoke, "The only thing I said was consider it dropped."

"But you steady running your mouth. Shut the hell up, means shut the hell up please. When I say drop it that is what I mean. Now leave me alone and don't say another word about my children."

I got in bed, and he began to walk out. I mumbled as I turned my back, "All because of those grown kids."

Seconds later, my bedroom door slammed. I jerked up and stared. Marcus was standing in the room I yelled, "What is wrong with you!"

Standing at the foot of my bed he spoke in an inaudible, "What did you just say?"

"What?"

"I walked out the room to get away and I heard you mumble under your breath. I heard it. I just want you to repeat it."

"I said all because of those grown kids."

Shaking his head in a yes form he spoke with an attitude, "That's what I thought you said."

Marcus reached under the cover. His hand grabbed my foot. I yelled in a question type, "What are you doing! What are you doing!"

"I'm washing your mouth out with soap."

"What!"

At this point, my body made a thumping sound onto the carpet floor as he pulled me out the bed. He literally began dragging me across the room. I could feel the carpet burns as I kicked at him to lose my foot. His grip was tighter than ever, as we got to the bathroom door of our bedroom door. I kicked harder and harder, but he continued to hold my foot. Being smart Marcus opened the top with one

hand. Somehow, he overpowered me and was

facing me. I moved my head back and forth as my

arms were swinging violently so he could not do

as he wanted but no luck. He took one of his

hands and held my arm as he began to pour the

liquid all onto my face with some getting in my

mouth. I couldn't defend my face properly. I

began to choke from the soap. He got up and

spoke with deep breaths, "Now go and wash your

mouth out."

Still stunned from the actions that just

happened, he stopped short from the door to say,

"And this time keep your mouth closed."

Like nothing ever happened, he left me on

the floor. I was hysterical and frustrated.

Honestly, I was in surprise this disagreement

went that far. Getting up off the floor, I stumbled

my way into the bathroom. I was

crying and didn't know what to think. It took a

few times but eventually all the soap was gone.

My hair was wet and so was my face from the

tears. My thoughts were beyond me as I replayed

the scene in my mind; in hope that I made a mistake.

Surely there is more to this than him being angry because I said, "those grown kids." I dried my face and washed my hair before changing gowns. I took a towel and washed the soap off the floor as much as possible. Climbing back into bed, I tried to go to sleep but couldn't. Marcus scared me so bad that I didn't know what to think by his actions.

About two hours later, I heard him ease in the room.

He got in the bed and asked, "Love you sleep?"

I didn't respond at once because I really didn't want to talk to him. He asked again, "Love, wake up."

Slowly turning around, I faced him as he said, "I'm sorry baby for what I did. Something as simple as that should not have caused me to get so angry but I told you to drop it, and you mumbled anyway."

My silence was golden. Marcus spoke, "Sarah please forgive me for acting like that. It didn't matter if you mumbled or not, I should not have gotten angry."

He gave me that sad look and I touched his face. Tears fell shortly as he said, "I don't like it that you all don't get along. I despise it so. I want my children and the woman I love to be a happy family, but it hasn't happened. I don't know what to do about it, but I am dealing with it to the best of my ability."

"I'm sure it will happen on time. We can't rush it. They have to have time to warm up to me. They are all older than I am and that could be a factor."

"I love you and I don't care about you being younger than they are. You are my wife, and you are my family, my future, my new life."

I towered Marcus as he said that with kisses as sweet as ever. He gave back to me the same feeling I was expressing as we tossed and turned in the bed with kisses. I could feel the love between us as we were making out in this way.

My love flipped me onto my stomach and entered my vagina. This way of making up was unique. He has never taken it from the back in the bed like this, but it was still wonderful all the same.

Though, the more I tried to move the more pressure he applied to me. The more he took me the more my fingers became interlocked with the sheet on the bed. Our lovemaking was surpassing any other times we've had together. Marcus was rough as he was trying out this new thing. The heat was to the max and I could literally feel the sweat dripping off his chest onto my back as he took me higher and higher. Every pounding time, he entered me our bodies would stick. When he pulls back to pound again, our bodies made that sticking sound.

Now sweat is dripping from my head as I bury my face in the warm bed to wipe away the heated seduction. My husband was so in tuned with my body that my orgasm came in multiple ripples I hollered for him. On cue his mouth shouted, "You mine."

With me on my stomach smiling, he waited until his breathing was normal before removing his clingy, oily male stick from my swollen but moist vagina. Marcus gave my butt a loud smack and we laughed. He lies beside me and puts his arm around me. We didn't wipe off and I couldn't move for his hammering was still being felt. His breath murmured, "I love you Sarah, God how I love every inch of you Sarah."

Snuggling a little bit closer, I responded with so much joy "I love you too Marcus. Good night, babe."

Chapter 3

Getting up and going to work was hard. When that alarm sounded, I wanted to hit the snooze but knew if I did the kids weren't going to be taught today by me.

Turning over, I saw Marcus was still asleep. Giving him a peck he spoke in a tired pitch, "Good morning, love."

I was surprised that he was alert. Giving him another peck I replied, "Good morning to you too."

Going with my usual routine, I got up and showered. Soon as I was finished getting ready, I took another look at him and giggled. With his eyes still closed my husband said, "I know why you are laughing?"

"And why am I laughing?"

He smiled in his speech when he spoke, "Because of those back-to-back orgasms I did."

I could only laugh more for he was right. Remembering my stop, I said before leaving, "When I get off, I am going to stop by Sharon's."

He turned over and said, "That'll be fine. I'm glad you are going to go by there."

"What you have planned for today?"

With his eyes still closed and groggy in speech, he replied, "Doing some research material for the upcoming seminars."

"Oh yeah, I forgot about that."

"Yup, my day is planned if I could ever recuperate from your loving."

I gave him a kiss and said, "Got to go. Love you."

"Love you too."

Today I am going to work with a chuckle and an outward manifestation that only God, Marcus and my body knows. When I arrived at work, everything was smooth. My entire higher math classes were great. I was moving along so that it never occurred to me that the day was about over. We were back to being us as if last night never happened. For the most I was still happy and also curious to go by Sharon's house. I don't know what she wants or what she could possibly have to say that I would want to hear. But not to disappoint my love, I plan to drop in anyway. Just before my day ended, I got a set of white and red roses. The arrangement was wonderful and one of the best I have ever seen.

The only thing on the card was my name but I didn't need one to know who it was from. My co-workers admired the arrangement as they smelled the roses like I did. Seeing this set up, made me more anxious to get home. Placing my beautiful flowers on the floorboard, I called Marcus, but he did not pick up, so I left a message that I was on my way to see his kid's mom. Silently I drove almost seven miles to Sharon's. I prayed she was gone. I blew the horn and as luck would have it Sharon came to the porch waving for me to get out.

Being polite I spoke, "Hello" as if I meant it while shutting my car door.

Cheerfully she replied, "Come on in Sarah bug."

I walked rapidly as she asked, "How was your day?"

"Great how was yours?"

"It was nice and thanks for dropping by."

She opened the front door and stood to the side. I walked through and waited for her. She asked, "Want me to hang your jacket up?"

"That will be nice."

She closed the front door. I handed her my jacket as she pointed towards a seat to say, "Grab a seat."

I sat down facing the door. Before she sat down, she asked, "You want a drink or tea possibly?"

"No, I'm fine thank you, but I would like to get to the point. I just got off from work and would like to get home as soon as I can."

"Most definitely. I can understand your position. I want to talk to you about Marcus."

A red light flashed. I knew it, I thought as I asked nicely as possible, "What about him?"

"I don't know what all he had told you about our divorce."

"Sharon," I cut her off.

"Yes, Sarah bug?"

"I don't think I should be having this conversation with you. Whatever happened between you two was between you two. Nothing was on my end about your marriage falling apart."

As Sharon was being the same ole Sharon, she smiled deviously as she spoke, "No but you helped it right along."

"How is that?"

"We discussed getting back together, until you showed up or you did not know about it."

I didn't know, and it really didn't matter. Marcus and I are married and for whatever reason he didn't make it work I didn't care. Making sure I say the right words, I stated calmly as I could, "I ran into him at the coffee shop on my way to work. I had no idea I would ever see him again after my graduation, but I did. I am not a home wrecker, but you can believe what you choose."

She didn't like my answer. I could see it on her face. She said with evil, "I wanted you over here so we could talk woman to woman. You are the stepmother of my children, and you are married to the man I have loved for about forty years or more. Surely you should listen to what I have to say, I had Marcus first."

Those last four words put a sour taste in my mouth. Taking a deep breath, I spoke, "Yes you do have children older than me, but I am not your child. I am YOUR EX-HUSBAND'S WIFE."

Sharon stared at me as I stated that to her. Licking her lips and sighing as to calm herself she spoke, "Let us start over. I want you and my girls to get along and that is the main reason for this gathering today, but I see now you need to know some things."

With a little attitude I stated, "First things first, it's not my fault that we don't get along. They don't like me."

Her oldest daughters Katie and Tonya came in the room. I didn't like it because it didn't feel right. Having a smug look Sharon said, "You right they do not. They all wanted their parents to get back together and so did I. You are young and inexperienced. Marcus does not need someone like you."

"BUT HE HAS SOMEONE LIKE ME!" I yelled at her.

Sharon stood up and her daughters got beside her. Their mother said, "You may be his new bed mate, but I will always have his heart and his children. He married to you but when he goes out of town, I am with him and sleeping with him."

I almost blank out. I stared at her again as she spoke slower, "I am a housewife, and I can travel all over the world with Marcus. You have a job and can't. We spend a lot of steamy nights in the finest hotels money can buy. Why else do you think he only calls you by eight?"

When I didn't respond she said to make me angry, "Because by eight o' five he's inside of me."

Reaching for her was impossible because her daughters kept pushing me back towards the front door. I even tried to fight them, but they were not trying to fight. They were only restraining me from getting to Sharon and that was odd. I didn't care I wanted her and those daughters of hers. Screaming loudly, "Let me go! Let me go! Come on let's settle this like women. Tell your daughters to move out the way so I can get to you."

She laughed as she waved her hand towards me. Her daughters literally pushed me out the front door and I landed onto the porch. They laughed as they threw my jacket out at me. I wanted to hit on the door. I knew they could call the police, and I could go to jail for trespassing and lose all my certifications. She was not worth that. They were not worth it.

Rushing to my car I fired it up, backed out and began to call Marcus. He finally answered. I screamed, "Tell me it's not so! You need to tell me RIGHT NOW! It isn't so!"

"What are you talking about?"

Tears were in my voice as I couldn't imagine him being unfaithful to me. He spoke clearly, "Sarah calms down and talk to me."

I hung up and did not want to talk about it. I want to see his face when I tell him what she told me. Driving fast, I made it home quickly. Soon as I pulled up, he opened the kitchen door and stood there. I snatched the gear in park, rapidly turned off the switch, slammed the car door and ran to him hitting him in the chest with my fist. He threw me on the floor and braced himself on top of me. He yelled, "What's gotten in to you! What's wrong with you!"

Tears were all on me as I spoke as much as I could, "Sharon told me she been going with you on your business travels and sleeping with you. Is it true?"

He looked at me in such a way that said is that what this is all about? He spoke, "That's nothing to get upset about. She goes when I go to a city her family is in. She has her own room, and we do not see each other until it is time to leave."

I stared at him angrily as I said, "She didn't tell me to come over there for anything."

"What do you think?" he said with an attitude.

"It's not what I think! Have you been sleeping with your ex-wife!"

He gave his eyes a roll before saying, "The last time I had sex with her was right before I met you. Since then, I haven't touched her. She would not say such a lie about me and her."

Marcus is taking up for her as I stated, "Your daughters were there, and they can vouch for it."

He turned his nose up as he said, "My daughters would not agree to such a thing."

"I am telling you they were there and if they have Jesus, they will tell the truth!

"Now let me up!"

He turned his head from me, then looked at me as he spoke, "If I let you up, you will behave?"

I was quiet. He asked again, "If I let you up, will you behave?"

"Yes," I almost screamed.

Marcus let me up and helped me off the floor before leading me to the living room. He stood a few feet in front of me as I asked angrily, "Why didn't you tell me?"

"I didn't think it was important. I have known this woman for over forty years or so and I do in some form love her but it's not like ours. I have children by her, and we do have grandchildren. When we got together you said you understood my relationship with Sharon and now you act like you don't."

"Marcus, she called me to her house, just to tell me she is sleeping with you. How do you think I am to take that news?"

My husband laughed as he replied, "With a laugh because I barely can handle you, why would I make love to Sharon and come home to ravish you?"

I didn't say anything. He touched my hands and spoke, "I love you Mrs. Sarah Grady. I admit I should have told you, but we won't have to worry about her going on any more trips. Is that ok?"

"It's okay," I said as if I was really not convinced.

Marcus gave me a hug to say, "Today I resigned."

My head jerked as I stammer, "You what?"

With his hands resting on my shoulders, he leaned back to say, "I resigned because I want to spend a lot of time with my young wife. We have money so living as we always have is not an option. We can still take trips and go traveling in the summer and nights out on the weekend if we want."

"You did all that for me?"

"Yes. I want to be here for you whenever you need me. I was not all that great of a husband

61

to Sharon because we did not have money like I do now. I can't change the past, but it is here with you that I make my future."

Reaching up, I hugged my husband. He held me as I said, "I am sorry I flew in at you with such rage."

"It is understandable."

Deciding that the time was right I said, "I also don't want to attend that church anymore."

He released me and asked, "What has the church done to you?"

"Nothing. Your old family attends it, and I don't want to be near them if I don't have to."

"My old family?"

"Let me be more specific. I don't want to go to the church that the ex-wife and children attend. They don't like me and after today I don't care to see them either. I'm sorry but I've had it up to here with them and how they treat me when you are not looking."

He stared at me as if I was speaking another language. I said it again, "I refuse to worship in a service where your ex-wife is there. I refuse to attend a meeting if your children are there for, they were there as they heard Sharon say those things to me. Did you not hear me?"

"Yes, I heard you, but you will go where I tell you to go. If I tell you, we are going there for worship that is where we are going. I am the man, and I run this household not you."

I stood there as he spoke in a more reasonable tone, "We will discuss this matter later."

His cell phone text message read out loudly, "It's Katie, its Katie." He touched the screen, and I heard my voice. Going to his side, I saw his daughters standing in front of me and not pushing me as they were; then I saw Sharon. She looked frightened. He closed it and almost demanded "Why didn't you tell me you attacked Sharon?"

"Attack her? She had a smirk on her face. She was taunting me about sleeping with you."

"That is not what it looked like to me."

"I know what it looked like, but I promise it wasn't like that. I think you should call Sharon and confront her on her lies; even call your two daughters they were there. That's if they don't lie about it."

Having a smug look I heard him say, "I sure will."

I went outside to get my briefcase and vase of flowers out the car. I wasn't gone long. Soon as I used my foot to close the door, I heard him say. "You should not have told her that. You know how young girls take things and run."

He laughed and said, "Bye Love."

He turned back around and saw me standing there. I asked, "Why are you are calling her Love?"

"I call everyone Love."

"No. Love is the pet's name you have for me and only me."

"So, I can't call my children that either?"

"You know what I mean?"

"No, I don't know what you mean. My children have nothing to do with what we are talking about."

I almost pleaded when I said, "They lie to you, and you believe them over me."

"They are my children. What will be their gain for lying?"

"They could have their parents together for their lies. I just can't believe you believe them while I am your wife."

"You are my wife, and you may not always be my wife, but they will always be my children."

My mouth flew open. I stared at him to say, "Maybe you need your old family back and not your new one."

"Sarah you are my family, and I love you but don't make me chose between you and them."

"It's not about choosing. It's about who is right and I have been right Marcus."

He spoke with modesty, "Yeah and they say the same thing."

"I admit it has not been easy but if we love like we should love, we can overcome this. I told the Lord that I will love you through everything, is this not included?"

"Yes."

His phone rang again and this time it was his daughter Tonya. He put her on speaker and said as he looked at me in a picking form, "Hello my Love."

"Daddy, how are you doing?"

"I'm good."

"I want to tell you first that Sarah came over here with an attitude. I didn't like the way she was talking to momma and if you don't do something about it I will."

I, in dismay continued to stand in the same spot, astounded. He lifted his finger to silence me as he asked, "She had an attitude?"

"She did. We had to stand in front of momma. I couldn't believe her actions."

"Why was she going after your mother?"

Chapter 4

"I don't know. We came in just in time to stop her. Momma was terrified of Sarah. I have never known her to act like that. You said she is nice but so far, I can't believe it. The worst part is I don't think you need someone like her in your life. I am afraid of what she could do to you."

Focusing on me, he spoke, "Love, I am not worried about that. Sarah is sweet."

"Daddy she is a fake."

Tears began to fall a little as I listened to him in part agree with his daughter.

My husband stated, "I love her Tonya, and I know she loves me."

Sounding disappointed his daughter said, "You've known mom longer and y'all have a history that goes back when you both were about ten or more. Don't you still love mom?"

When she asked that he turned the speaker off. I felt defeated in my own home by his old family. Marcus got up and walked outside. My heart is racing because I wanted to hear what he was going to tell her, but he didn't let me. He came back inside and slanted himself on the door frame. I would not look at him. Many emotions were flooding me, and I don't know which one would be the right one, so I continued to sit with my head down.

He called my name, but I didn't answer at first. With my eyes still focused on the flowers I paused before asking, "Why did you go outside? I wanted to hear what you had to tell her."

"I told her the truth."

Making up my mind to play the guilt trip like she did I sounded sad when I spoke, "How do I know? You went outside and I could not hear you."

"Trust me I told the truth."

I looked up and asked, "Which was?"

"What we already talked about?"

I asked him again, "Which was?"

The love of my life said, "I believe you did make a go at Sharon."

Flatly my tone said, "That's all?"

"That is all I saw on the tape."

"What about what I told you she said?"

"It's possible."

A question came on my face as I asked flatly, "Possible?"

"Yes possible."

"Then how did I know she was going out of town with you?"

"She told you; I have no doubt about that."

"But you don't believe the rest or what I have said to you?"

"I didn't say I didn't believe it. I said it was feasible."

"Feasible?"

He said it again, "Feasible."

Plainly I stated, "Tell me you believe me."

To patronize me he said, "I believe you and I thought you should know that your prayers have been answered."

"What prayers?"

"My daughters and Sharon are moving out of state to her sister's. You should be jumping up for joy right now. It's not like you like the girls anyway."

"It's not that I don't like them, they don't like me."

"Well, my grandchildren are leaving too, and they don't have anything to do with it. Now I only have you and that should make you happy."

Marcus was getting angry and this time I noticed it. To soften the conversation, I gave him that smile he loves to see as I spoke, "I love the roses."

"I do as well but who bought them for you?"

Laughing I placed them down on the table and walked over to him. He asked more demanding, "Who bought them?"

"You did. Who else knows the flowers I love so much?"

Walking up on me, his words were not kind, "Hoping you would tell me. Could be Mr.

Goss that teacher from your job; you know my daughter's ex?"

Seeing that he was indeed serious I asked, "You mean you didn't send them?"

"No. I've been in this house all day preparing seminars fast as I can just to be with you."

Looking at the flowers, I said, "Well Marcus, I don't know who sent them if you didn't."

"You better give me an answer. I am beginning to believe that you know more than you say."

This time I stared at him to ask, "What are you implying?"

"I am not implying anything. I am going by what I see and that is a vase full of expensive roses in my wife's hand. By the way she can't tell me who bought them."

Being as honest as I could I exclaimed, "It's because I don't know. I told you. I thought you bought them. If another man

71

bought them, why would I bring them home for my husband to see?"

Using questions in his tone, he whispered loud enough for me to feel fearful, "What else have you been getting rid of, while I am away? Who are you sleeping with? Was the baby mine you lost?"

"Huh?"

"You heard me. I think you forgot I was home and wanted to enjoy them before I got back."

"That is not true. My allegiance is with you and our marriage."

"Really?" Marcus said, as he stared.

I backed up and was stopped by the coffee table. He put his face close to mine.

I could smell liquor. Pulling my face away from his, I whispered, "Have you been drinking and that is why you could not answer the phone when I called earlier?"

"I'm grown and I don't have to answer to you. Now tell me what you been doing?"

"I am not lying. I haven't been doing anything. My love is for you and only you," I stated again.

His face became almost my face; for that is how close our faces were. I dared to breathe. His tone got louder when he spoke the word, "Really."

I shook my head, no. He moved like he was walking off. He took two steps then instantly he turned around and hit me with all his strength. His hand touched his knees as my body did a complete spin. I landed on the coffee table, causing it to be broken in half. I didn't get a chance to get my senses together before Marcus picked me yelling, "Liar! You are a cheater and a liar!"

As loud as I could, I screamed "Marcus, love don't."

But he did. He threw my body into the wall and the sheet rock broke. He hit me in my mouth and my teeth rattled. I can taste the blood as I fell to the living room tile floor. The pain shot over my entire skeleton frame. Before I could gather my senses, he snatched me up again and this time he used my body as a pole by ramming my head into another part of the sheet rock. That wasn't enough, so he threw me again and this time breaking the huge mirror that hung on the wall. The pieces shattered all around me. My skin was burning because I knew I had gotten cut from the glass.

Marcus picked me up and threw me against the other wall. I was trying to defend myself as he came after me. This time I hit him in the stomach. He bent down and came up with an upper cup to my chin. I fell and he picked me up screaming, "Didn't your momma tell you to keep your hands to yourself!"

He hit me a few more times in the face with his right hand. Marcus must have seen that I have had enough because he dropped me. I was fearful to even move. He left out. I started to get up but couldn't. Ten minutes later, he came back to help me to the couch. I could see blood all over me from my nose and my lip.

He started crying and I didn't care about him crying. He just jumped on me about nothing. He dried his face and said, "Love you bleeding."

I continued to sit there, shocked. Marcus left out then came back with a cold towel. He wiped away the blood from my face. When he got to my arm he spoke kindly, "Love you may need stitches."

Allowing my eyes to glance down at my arm; it had a huge gash. I felt weak at the sight. He left me alone then came back to clean my cut with iodine. He placed a white bandage over it and before wrapping it. I glimpsed up at him and he stated, "Love, I lost it, and I know you won't forgive me."

What he was saying did not register to me. My nerves were scattering as he touched me. Altogether I needed to run, he sensed it. His hands being lovingly on me, is the last thing I needed. He spoke, politely, "Don't leave me Sarah. You all I have now. My girls are leaving and it's only you and I."

I didn't answer. In a demanding statement, his words were, "Tell me you won't leave me."

Here I am wounded, frightened, a nervous wreck and all he can think about is me not leaving him. I could not look at him. I refused to look at him. My husband saw that I was not paying any attention to him, he grabbed my sore arm. I screamed.

Like a mad man applying pressure he asked in monotone, "You going to leave me?"

Marcus was making my arm ache worse. Tears fell on me. I would have yelled out anything at this point, as I announced loudly, "No. I'm not going to leave you. I love you."

He released my arm and spoke with the devil in his eyes, "Good because if you do, I will kill you. You hear me love. I will have to kill you and think no more about it."

When he spoke that sentence, I became petrified. For the last two days, my love has proven actions that are unlike him. Part of me is still horrified and the other half thinks it is a dream. No man has ever beaten on me before and no man has ever made me feel the way he makes me feel before. I called myself taking my time for love, to make sure I didn't fall into traps that I have heard my girlfriends in college talk about. One told me that her cousin Holly was involved with a man that beats her for the simple things.

Another one told how controlling her dad was to her mom and how he was never satisfied. What got me was how they both said, the end was death. They told me how the men would be sweet; then the next, flared with jealousy. To me that was not love but sure enough, I find myself facing what seems like the same dilemma I had only heard about. Marcus broke my thoughts by getting up to fix me a drink. He came back and handed it to me. I swallowed it completely.

My husband placed his head on my lap and cried. I could only pat his head and hope he doesn't do this again. One way or another I awoke to strange sounds. I lifted my head up and had not realized that I had fallen asleep on the couch and was covered up. There is no telling how long they been here because when I came to, people were walking out the door. It's funny how the house looked like nothing ever happened to it. I wanted to get up, but my body was raked with pain. My face felt swollen by my mouth, so I touched it and screeched.

He heard me and came to kneel beside me to say, "I called the school and talked to your principal. I told him you had an unexpected illness and will be out for the rest of the month. He was fine with it and told me to tell you to have an excuse and he hopes you get to feeling better."

My facial expression was in astonishment. My love spoke, "I have a friend at the doctor's office, and I have your excuse already. I've already put it in your purse, so you won't forget."

I didn't say a word. I didn't trust my own voice. Marcus said, "Love I need you to listen to me for a minute."

He admitted with love "I did buy the flowers. I got drunk and forgot. It wasn't until I saw the order for them charged to my Master Card. You mad?"

What is the point of being mad? It will only make things worse so I'm perfecting a career in lying as I spoke, "No, we all make mistakes, and this is just one of them."

"Thank you Love for being understanding."

I tried to get up and he helped me. With humor, he said, "You are probably sore."

Ignoring him, I vaguely asked, "I want to see a mirror."

He got my small one out my room and handed it to me. My face was a wreck and not only that, I had a tooth missing on the side. I wanted to scream and cry.

Marcus tried to make me feel better when he spoke, "Love I made you a dentist appointment and they are going to fix that by putting a partial."

Emotions were all upon me as I cried. He began to promise, "Sarah my Love I won't do this to you again. I should have had proof, but I snapped at the idea of another man being with you while I am away."

I did not say another word as he directed me with a statement, "Lie down and get more rest."

During this time, I don't know what to think or do. My thoughts rambled how it never occurred to me what I would do if a man put his hands on me.

Nevertheless, a husband. Never in all my days have I endured such embarrassment, injury, and inward humiliation. I could have any man I wanted but here I am with a man that is showing love by beating on me. Parts of me don't think he will change but my love for him must make him change. We've had more good times than bad so I can't let this get me down.

Forgetting my thoughts, I saw my cell on the floor as I asked nicely, "May I have a drink please?"

"The world for you my love" he got up and went in the kitchen. He brought me a coke on ice. I smiled for it is the little things he does or remembers that makes hard times bearable. "Here you go love," Marcus spoke as he handed it to me.

I gulped the soda down fast. He chuckled because I didn't realize how thirsty I was. I handed the glass back to him. Marcus looked around to say, "I had the house repaired while you slept. You like it?"

"I do. I like it a lot."

"What you want to do today?"

Very slowly, I replied, "Rest. I just want to rest."

"You go on and rest while I get dinner ready for you."

"Thank you."

He went in the kitchen. I picked up my cell and saw I had a message. It was from Mr. Goss. His text said that he heard I was going to be out for the remainder of the month, and he hopes all is well with me. Quickly I erased that text. It means nothing but after what I just went through, I don't need any hope you feel better texts from anyone. Placing my phone back to where it was, I laid down. Moments later my love came in and picked up my cell. He opened it and asked, "Have you been in your cell?"

I pretended not to hear him as he continued, "I had your cell set a certain way and I was wondering if you been in it?"

"I did. I saw I had texts from my co-workers wishing me well."

"I know I saw them too."

Panic filled me like that coke did. I glanced up at him as he said, "Because you don't like to mind. I am stripping you of your name. No longer will you be called Sarah. You will be called Child."

"Child?" I questioned.

Having a mean approach, his words were, "You have a problem with that?"

"No. What am I to call you?"

"Mr. Grady will be fine."

"How long is this to last?"

"Until I think you know how to listen to instructions. You were to lie down and rest and not be up checking your phone. Doing things like that makes me suspicious of your behavior."

"What is wrong with me checking my phone? I am not doing anything I shouldn't be."

"I believe you aren't doing anything but after last night, everything is new to me. Go on and rest. Dinner will be ready shortly."

Following instructions like a good girl, I lay down and went to sleep. I don't know how long I was asleep, but I awoke to a sweet-smelling aroma. Marcus came over to where I was. He extended his hand and spoke softly, "It's time for you to wash up and eat."

With a little help from him, I got up and went to the bathroom. I got in the shower and began to cry delicately. I was making sure I muffled my pain and would have cried longer but he knocked on the shower glass doors. I jumped and he saw it. Marcus opened the doors and said, "You don't have to worry about me doing that to you again. I was wrong, foolish and I apologized for it."

Remembering what he said, I replied, "Ok, Mr. Grady."

He gave me a smile when he said, "You are a fast learner. I like that."

He left me alone. I wanted to run away like the water down the drain but know all too well that you can't run away from a problem; you must face it. I got out the shower, I dried off. Marcus was sitting on the edge of the bed. I instantly sensed fear when he spoke, "Come here. I'm not going to hurt you."

Chapter 5

Walking slowly towards him, he noticed how I was somewhat frightful. This time he put more emphasis in his tone by screaming, "Get over here! I said I was not going to do that to you, but you make a man like me do this type of stuff to you. At least Sharon knew how to obey."

Just hearing her name made me furious. I didn't know how close I was to him when I yelled back, "I am not your ex-wife! I am who I am."

He snatched me around and with his oversized hand to place it under my throat as he downed me on the soft fluffy bed. The look in his eyes was that of evil at its finest. My hands flew up to protect me, but he had them both covered with his right arm. He started laughing while I am in terror. Out of nowhere, he smiled and spoke, "See I was playing with you, but you were looking all serious. I had to laugh and let you up."

I was still shaking from the small attack as he laughed more and helped me up.

He grinned nicely this time, to say "Come on Child, it's time to eat then make up."

He led me as if he was taking me to a dance floor to dance. I had no choice but to obey. When we got to the kitchen, he had ordered Chinese take-out. Sounding surprised I asked very gentle, "I didn't know they delivered all the way out here in the country?"

"They don't but the owner owed me a favor, so he brought it out here for us to enjoy."

I didn't know what to say because he knows I don't care for Chinese; it's his favorite food. Trying to be lovely, I smiled warmly as he pulled the chair out for me. I sat and scooted to the table. He got on the opposite side and fixed our plates. He gave me that look that continues to melt away any fury I may feel towards him. There next to him, I saw our cell phones. I wondered why he has my phone. He has never had my phone until now. Forgetting all about his reasons for doing anything, I waited until he was settled in his seat before asking, "Where are your girls moving too?"

He looked up and gave me a warm feeling of love as he spoke, "I'm glad you asked. They are moving to Augusta, Georgia. I had talked to Elisabeth and told her we plan to come for a visit. She was delighted."

"It's lovely out there this time of year. Do you remember when we visited there?"

Marcus took a swallow of wine as replied, "Yes, love. We stayed in the hotel for three days, making love and watching TV. Don't I remember those times we spend together."

Laughing with real humor, he stated, "I love when we go traveling. There is so much we can see and do."

"I know and that time will come for us to do that again."

"I would love to take the grand children to Six Flags and Disney World this year. I will be just you, me and our grandchildren at Elisabeth's house."

I didn't like that last part, but I made sure not to show the face of displeasure. He began eating his food; I, on the other hand, watched him with semi-joy. He looked up and saw me not eating. He asked, "Eat, your food is getting cold, Child."

With no more trying to pass time, I ate the food with disgust. Soon as I was almost finished, he asked, "I thought you didn't like Chinese?"

"I don't but you graciously ordered it and fixed it. My mom always told me to eat food that is placed before you."

"Speaking of family, I talked to your brother. I told him you were sleep and you will call him later. He bought it and we hung up."

He ate more as my eyes lit up at the sound of my brother's name. I thought about how he seldom talks about my family since, his attitude has changed. It wasn't until his persona became altered that I found out that he only tolerates Sam, and he wants to be the only man around me. Sometimes, Marcus gives me the blues when I talk to anyone but him. He puts up with the fact that I work, and I communicate with my co-workers. There have been instances, where he would go to work with me, sit in my classes and observe.

It was ok for him to do that because of his profession, and no one thought it strange. They didn't know that he does that so I can only talk to him and no one else. During this smothering time, I almost forgot how I sounded to other people because I didn't talk to anyone. Not only that, when I talk to anyone, the phone had to be on speaker. He would pretend not to listen but soon as I would hang up, I got the third degree. He would go on seminars, then return to check my phone records and wanting to know what all we talked about.

Don't let him call me and I didn't answer, he would ask a million questions. Many of the times, I would be at work and cannot answer the phone in class. He got smarter and started texting or calling between the bells. When I got off from work, he was calling, and we would talk until it was time for me to go to sleep. Basically, he would be the first and last voice I heard every morning and night. In the beginning I believed it was cute until it got serious. The more I think about it, the signs of abuse were in play; I didn't recognize it not because I had not ever been in it until now. The sound of the glass jumping startled me.

Marcus screamed, "What you thinking about!"

Being distressed, I responded quickly, "I just thought about my brother and how I haven't talked to him in a while."

Between his teeth, he gritted his sentence in a lowly manner, "When I am with you, like I am now; you are to keep your mind on what I am saying and doing. Is that clear, Child?"

"Yes, Mr. Grady."

Marcus gave me a long stare that sent chills to my mother's grave. The butterflies in my stomach began flying into each other as he glared longer at me. The sweat on my head refused to drip as he continued to give me that evil glare. Thank God, my cell rung loudly. He picked it up and threw it to me. It was my brother Sam. He glanced at me then said, "Answer it and keep it short."

Touching the talk button, I put it on speaker and spoke kind of lively, "Hello."

"Hey sis, how you doing?"

It was great to hear his voice. I almost cried but I remembered I had to keep my answers brief and conversation short; therefore, I reply with a pause, "I'm good, how about you?"

"I'm great, thanks. I called your job today before I talked to Marcus on your cell phone."

"Why you call my job?"

"Other than I haven't had time to run by your house, you quit answering your cell and I don't know Marcus's number. He changed it or I've been dialing the wrong number."

That didn't sound right. How was he calling me and I didn't have a missed call. I stopped questioning myself as Marcus gave me that grin; of letting me know he has been intercepting my phone calls and God knows what else. Remembering he made a statement, I replied with speed, "Oh, someone kept calling so he changed it, I believe."

"Well, sis I haven't heard from you, and I was worried."

Making myself do a fake laugh, I stated, "I'm good, Sam. Mr. I mean Marcus and I are great, we just been in our own little world."

"Am I on speaker because I hear an echo?"

"Yeah, my phone doesn't pick up too well in the house and when it does, I put it on speaker."

"You might need a new phone. What happened to it?"

"I dropped it in water."

"Oh, ok that explains that."

The line was silent as Marcus gave me a warning sign to hang up quickly. I asked Sam, "So you called the school?"

"Yeah, your boss said you were sick. What is wrong with you?"

"Running a fever and coughing for a little while."

"You haven't seen anyone about your fever and coughing? Do you have the funds to see a doctor because this isn't like you at all?"

"Yes! We have money. It just started and I wanted to make sure, I don't give this coughing to anyone."

"I'm just saying because we all need help sometimes and if you guys don't have it, let me know. I am your brother."

"Sam, I work and so does Marcus. I still have a hefty portion of my inheritance left."

He laughed and said, "I am your brother, and I hope you would tell me if something was wrong."

"I would. You're family."

"Let me know what the doctor says when you go."

"Okay."

"I take it you can't talk right now because of the short answers?"

"I am sick," I added flatly with a cough.

He laughed and said, "You right, I forgot all about it. Go to bed and I will keep a check on you. If you haven't heard from me in a day or so, call me back."

"Ok."

"Goodnight Sarai. I love you."

"Goodnight Samuel, Sam. I love you too."

It was great to call him that pet name, we both had since children. I hung up and Marcus extended his hand for me to give him back my phone. Which, I did. Soon as he got my phone he stated, "So he thinks we broke."

"I never gave him any indication that we were struggling in any form because we are not."

"He must have gotten it from somewhere."

"I don't know where from, but I can ask him."

The rise and fall of his chest showed me that he was getting a fever in his feelings. I tried to ease the moment when I said, "Mr. Grady, I have not signified any such a thing. I promise I haven't."

"I'm not blind. I've seen the way you use to look down your nose at my children and their mother."

Using his right index finger, he extended his hand and pointed towards the bedroom and stated, "Go in the room, I'm going to start teaching you how to survive the old fashion way; since you were born into a little money."

I got up and started to pick up my plate and he demanded, "Did I tell you to clean your area?"

"No," I spoke with assurance.

He stood up and said, "I told you to go to the room."

Putting the plate back onto the table, I went in the room. I had no idea what was coming but something told me to post up in the corner by the bathroom. He came in the room and looked at me before closing the door and turning off the lights. Marcus has never done this before as I began to shake. My Love has become skilled at making me afraid. I swallowed hard as his voice teased spookily and spitefully with the words, "I can see you, Child. Use your eyes to see me back."

In fact, I couldn't see him and that made me uncomfortable and terrified. I wanted to swing in the dark but didn't know what he would do if I hit him. The heart in my chest began speeding as my eyes grew bigger to see. Wham, wham, wham! From out of nowhere the fists attacked me. I fell backwards and slid down the wall. There is no need to fight back. I learned that standing up to him only entices his anger. Each time he hit me I could see a bright orange flash in the night. Soon as the sparkles stop, I could hear him walking off lightly when he said, "Stand back to your feet and fight."

I found strength and stood back to my feet. I've come to realize that he is attacking me in the dark gives him the perfect opportunity to beat me. Then I heard his voice on the other side of the room that said, "I'm teaching you how to fight with your senses."

Seconds later, Wham! Wham! Wham! Wham! His fist shook my head from side to side. I got angry and began swinging as I hit him a few times. Once I felt those connecting hits to him, I stopped swinging and fear took over. He hit me again. This time, my heart raced as I swung more and more on him. Then he was gone. Suddenly not too far from me, he stated, "See that was good. You are learning how to fight."

He turned the lights on. I saw that he was bleeding from his lip. He touched his mouth. A devious smile was seen as he spoke cockily, "You know I let you hit me, right?"

I didn't say a word as he turned the lights back off. Before I realized what happened, his fists had made connections to my face and body from various angles. I was swinging and swinging but I was losing. He was making power punches one after the other, with each punch more powerful than the last. Not able to take it anymore, I cried out in pain. His breathing was rough when he yelled, "Shut up and fight! Shut up and fight!"

Before the next scream could escape my lips, he hit me in the already aching and swollen mouth. I shut up and laid there as he hit me all in my breast and stomach area. I fell down and decided to lay there and not get up. Seconds later the attack stops, and the door opened and closed. I laid there begging God inside my mind and no answer still. Moments went by. I did not hear a door open, but he turned the lights on and asked, "You, ok?"

My body rakes with pain, he did this to me and all he can do was asked if I were ok? I tried to play it off as I responded, "I'm ok."

He came over and helped me up. I didn't know one could feel so many emotions at once. I groaned and he spoke softly, "Lay down."

I got in the bed, and he took off my clothes. Rubbing his hand lightly over my skin caused me to feel tingles. He whispered, "You know you beautiful. Your breast is the perfect size, and I love every inch of you."

Words could not come out. The entire time he is talking, I am trying to figure out what is happening in my life. Breaking my thoughts was the mouth of my husband on my breast. He was turning me on, and I didn't get it. I should still be upset right now but I am not. I am allowing him to please me as sighs fled my mouth like someone running away. Consciously my body wants him while unconsciously I don't, but I can't help it. If I fake at this point, there is no telling what could happen, so I better like it. Truth be told, I was.

Chapter 6

Marcus got on the bed and got between my legs. This time, he placed my legs far beyond his head. I thought he was trying to break me in half. I was already in such agony; therefore, this new position was not bothering me. With the back of my thighs securely resting on his arms, he rushed the vagina with force a few times. Then he stopped inside me to let me feel the throbbing. When he pulled himself almost out, he reentered the long shaft slowly into me as to massage her or make up for the forceful entry.

I didn't know what to make of this. My vagina reacted on her own as she welcomed his long, thick meat stick. There was no way I should be this ready for a man that just beat me in the dark, but my body knows what it wants. The slower my love went in and out of me the more I craved what he was doing. This loving was a record level high and for each time he drove his pleasure friend into me the more I would squeeze onto him.

Each time he pulled back to tease the vagina; he would drive harder as to make her mind him and it was working. When he got the rhythm, he was searching for he started humping me harder and harder. I've never had a good pain like this before that made me insane with need. The more my love rolled his hind parts in a deep drawing circle, the more I wanted to move my hind part to him but could only do so much; for the position I was in. The deeper he went inside me the faster his speed became. Then he started saying softly, "Take that. Take that" and I was taking it for it was so good to me.

My legs were beginning to have a numbing sensation but that was short lived as his body was humping me so hard that I had the feeling of being broke in half. I had a short orgasm as my body felt helpless because the pain was overwhelming any great awareness I had in the beginning. I assumed he was about to release because he yelled out, "Don't you run pussy! Stay and fight."

When he said stay and fight, my mind went back to what just happened. I started feeling rigid and sad all over again. Silently I prayed; hurry up and he didn't. He began saying, "You behaved badly, so let me teach you a lesson."

I didn't understand this new way of intensity as my body shook from pleasure, over and over. He with his eyes closed appeared to be talking to himself while still being hard inside me. Finally, he said softly, "It's too good to me."

His body froze and I felt a huge throbbing at the end of his stick. He tried to push himself inside me in his semi-frozen state but couldn't. Taking long deep breaths, he finally eased out of me and my legs fell like a tree hitting the ground. Marcus got up and went to the bathroom. I couldn't feel my legs even if I tried. I could not move and didn't want to sort out the loving we just made so I closed my eyes.

I awoke the next morning to the smell of eggs and bacon. Doing my best, I moved and sat alongside the bed. Marcus came in and spoke, "Good morning, Child."

"Ooh, you startled me. Good morning Mr. Grady."

"I know it's almost noon but I'm cooking you breakfast."

I looked at the window and saw the sun was indeed high into the sky. I faced him and said, "Wow, thank you. I didn't know I had slept that long."

"You did. Your body needed the rest after the way we got it on last night."

"My body sure did need the rest," I said as I thought about the pain.

"Were you pleased like I was last night?"

"I did but it was the most different. You were like someone I never had before, and I only had you as a lover."

"You know why it was different?"

"No why?"

He gave me a sly grin and spoke happily, "I took a male enhancement that allowed me to ride you like I did. Not only that but the fight we had, made the makeup sex worth it. I am not lying. The sex was too good. I couldn't stop. I didn't want to stop. I hated that orgasm interrupted the punishing I was putting on you."

"Just take whatever it is you are taking and lets us not do that lesson part again."

"I don't know about that one Child. Since I retired, the fighting and makeup sex is almost what I look forward too."

I was learning not to say too much to him because of this new him and attitude. Sometimes I wouldn't even know when to do number one or two. He left out the room and I took a shower. When I dried off, I put on a pair of joggers and a tee shirt to match. Putting on my socks, I got my house shoes and went to the kitchen. The house was spotless, and the food did smell wonderful. He pointed to the chair at the table to say, "Grab a seat."

Taking a seat, he fixed my plate and said, "I'm doing my best to spoil you."

"It's working, Mr. Grady."

"Hurry up. You have a dentist appointment for the missing tooth."

With no more talking to him, I ate the food and drank the orange juice in haste. The fresh fruit was wonderful and on time. He was already dressed, and he drove me to the dentist. When we got there it was not packed. I was glad I didn't see anyone I knew. I reached for my cell phone and remembered he has it. Marcus gave me that smile and I waited for my name to be called. Once in the back, the dentist fitted the open space. He ordered it and told me to come back in three days. Marcus and I left the office and went back home. We made it inside and he stated, "I been thinking while you were letting that bastard in your mouth."

That stunned me. Silently I stated, "He is the dentist. The one you picked."

"I don't care he is still a man with a third leg like me."

Doing what I could to redirect the conversation, I asked politely and dreadfully, "What were you thinking Mr. Grady?"

"I want you to quit work."

"Quit what?"

A million things filled my mind, and quitting work was not one of them. He stated, "Yes, you are going to quit work and let me provide for us."

"Mr. Grady, I don't mind helping you."

"I know you don't, but I want to keep you in my sight at all times, and I can't do that with you in a classroom teaching underserved children."

My senses spun because I could not grasp being made to give up what I love. In all honesty, I was ready to go back to work. The job was going to be my vacation from him. It hasn't been like that, but he has become abusive; therefore, work was to be my home away from home. Not to give into my thoughts, I asked, "When you want me to do it?"

"Today because I already called your principal, but he wasn't in."

"Ok, I will call back later, if that will be alright with you?"

"That will be perfect."

"Want me to fix you some food, since you have been waiting on me?"

"No, we can go out later to eat. Would you like that?"

"Yes, I would love that Mr. Grady."

The loud ringing came from his phone rung. It usually tells who is calling but this time it didn't. He changed it. He got up and went to the back patio. I wanted to sneak and listen but wasn't quite sure if that was what I really wanted to do. Twenty minutes later he came back and said, "It was Katie. She needs me to send her a thousand dollars for her rent and electric bill because she hadn't gotten paid yet. What you think?"

My first choice was to say no but I know he worship his lying, deceitful children. I think he is testing me, so I replied, "Sure. Your daughter needs you and if you can help her do it. She is your daughter after all."

He gave me a sunshine smile. His voice was cheerful when he said, "I'm glad you said that. It means so much to hear that, Child."

"You want me to send it or you going to?" I asked in hopes to get out the house.

"You don't need to go outside Child. I will do it. You go on and fix a snack. When I get back, we can eat and watch a movie. Would you like that?"

"I would Mr. Grady."

He pitched me my phone and walked out the door. I placed the phone down, for I desperately wanted to call my brother Sam but knew better. I went in the kitchen to look for snacks. Moments later, the cell phone rung loudly, "It's me, It's me." He just left out. I have no idea as to why he is calling. Being jolly I stated, "Hello."

"What took you fifteen seconds to answer the phone?"

"I had walked off from it in search of snacks."

His tone changed, when he stated, "Oh. Put me on speaker so we can talk while you fix snack."

I put the phone on speaker and went back over to the fridge. I spoke, "Is there something in particular you would like?"

"Nothing specific, what you want?"

"We have cheese and crackers."

"No."

"Popcorn?"

"No."

"Raisin toast, orange slices and grape juice?"

"No."

"Let me see," I said as I pretended to look and open cabinet doors for sounds.

"Child, how about your favorite chocolate chip cookies and vanilla ice cream?"

Laughing like my old self, I replied, "That sounds good."

"Check and see if we have any."

I looked in the fridge and said, "I don't see any here. Let me go look in the deep freezer."

"Hurry up. I'm counting."

In lightning speed, I raced towards the utility room. Opening the lid, I saw the ice cream. I took it out and ran back to the kitchen area where the phone was. Sounding like I was out of breath, I replied, "We have some. I'm going to put it in the top of the fridge until you get home."

"What about the cookies? Do we have some cookies?"

"Let me run to the pantry."

Like before, I ran fast to the pantry. I looked on every shelf and didn't see the cookies. I raced back and heard Marcus say, "You have enough?"

The female said, "I don't."

"You want me to pay for that for you?"

"Could you please? I didn't bring enough money."

I spoke, "No cookies. You will have to bring them when you come."

It took him a few as he said, "No cookies?"

"No."

"I'll bring them."

Marcus hung up. I am wondering who is that he was talking too. I called him back. He didn't answer. Almost thirty minutes later he called and said, "I just sent the money off to Katie, but I will be a little late. I have an extra errand to run. Go on and eat what snack you have with you."

He hung up quickly and for some reason; I felt that he would be sleeping with this unnamed woman. Frustrated by everything, I ate the ice cream with no cookies. It is now nine o'clock. I wanted to call him but I know if he needs me, he will call me. Not sure what to do, the phone sounded, his ring tone. I dashed to it, but it was a text stating, he will be late and for me not to wait up. I replied, okay.

I washed my wounded arm and saw it was healing faster than I anticipated. My mind forgot all about my arm as it focused on Marcus and who the woman could be. I wanted to be angry, for my husband may be out with another woman. At the same time, if he's not here he is not abusing me or making me call him Mr. Grady. However, he's out with the voice I heard made me angrier than me calling him Mr. Grady. Who is she? I thought as sat on by the phone anticipating his next message that never came.

It's now eleven o'clock pm and no husband. I wanted to call him but reread his text instead. Whatever he is doing, it shouldn't take all night to do it. I got sleepy and fell asleep. I woke up and saw it was, two o'clock am and still no Marcus. I checked the phone and not even a text. I saw the empty corner in my bedroom and recalled when I was afraid of bad weather. I would sit in a corner, like my comfort zone.

Getting up out the bed, I sat in the corner and cried and cried. For some reason, crying felt better to me as I let whatever it is all out. My husband is abusive towards me since his retirement and now I think he is cheating. I wanted someone to talk to; then I thought about the Lord for he sees and hears all. With my head in my arms I said, "Lord, I hope you still hear me. I haven't been in your service in a while, but I don't know what to do. The preacher says to pray when we don't know our way and I don't understand why my husband had turned the way he has. I don't want to end up like the women I have heard about. Please God I don't want that to be my fate. I know that everything happens on your time, but I fear time could be running out for me. At least help me to understand what is happening so I can deal with it; in your name Jesus, Amen."

I lifted up my head to dry my eyes. When I sniffled, in my head, I heard, "Get away."

That voice spooked me. I looked around and thought someone must be in here with me but there was no one. I don't know why but I got up and began pacing the floor back and forth not sure of what to do. I decided to listen and rushed to the closet to get my traveling bag. When my eyes came across the bag, his car was heard by my ears pulling up. Fear set in as I raced to the kitchen table. Trying to calm my nerves, I placed my head on the table and pretended to be sleep. He came in through the kitchen and locked the door back. His steps towards me were lighter as I could hear him humming loudly. He rubbed my head of hair and spoke, "Wake up Child. It's time to go to bed."

Chapter 7

Acting groggy, I got up and he led me to the bedroom. I stripped off and got in the bed under him as if nothing was wrong. He held me and hummed in my ear as he fell asleep. The next morning, he was still in bed. I woke up and so did he. Being the concerned wife kicked in as I stated, "You had me worried last night. I didn't hear from you, and I didn't know what to think."

"You could have called. I would have answered."

"Where were you?" I gambled by asking.

He paused and said normally with a smile, "I tried this thing out. I had never done before in all my years."

"What thing you tried out?"

Marcus didn't pause or bat an eye as he stated, "I had a one-night stand and got my dick sucked."

I jumped up. I could feel him smiling as he stated nicely as to patronize me, "Child I wasn't cheating."

"Mr. Grady, yes you did."

"No, it's not. I did not enter her at any time."

He didn't finish it before he hollered, "She only, woo!"

I looked over at him when he said, "Come back to bed and let me tell you about it."

I stood there, and he removed the covers and held them up for me to get back in bed. I stood there and he spoke with tone, "Get in this bed now!"

Hurriedly, I got in. He fixed the covers on me. He said, "I met her at Wal-Mart. She didn't have enough change to pay for her things, so I offered. When I paid for them, I sent the money off and left. When I got outside, she was waiting on me. She asked if she could talk to me for a few. I said OK; that is when I text you about "a thing." I've never entertained having a woman down there on me and never thought of it, but she said, let me repay you for what you done. I told her that was okay, but she said she can make me feel good. I had just taken the male enhancement

115

before I left so I could be ready for you when we finished our snack, but it didn't happen like that. I asked to see her ID because I heard of stuff like this happening. She showed me her legal ID. She was nineteen to be exact. I took her to the nearest hotel, locked the door and got naked."

Parts of me didn't want to hear it but knew he was going to make me listen anyway, "Please don't make me listen to this."

"Child you must because you are my wife, and I don't have any secrets from you. If I honestly thought I was cheating on you I would not be telling you this, like this. But I don't consider this cheating on you, so I have nothing to hide."

I did not say a word. He spoke, "Anyway, I didn't know what to expect but she knew what she was doing. I lay on the bed, and she asked me if I ever had head before. I told her no. She said she really don't like to have sex on the first date, but she will do head because it is not sex. I agreed. She placed her small butt towards me. I was already ready for you as she put her mouth on my stick slowly. My toes wiggled."

He started smiling hard. I asked, "You still think it wasn't sex?"

"Child, I come to you and only you. Her doing that didn't mean crap to me but I have to tell you what happened. She went up and down with her mouth and worked my balls with her hands. I couldn't believe how good that was. I became out my mind and started playing in her with my fingers. The more my fingers wiggled the more out of control she got. I guess that enticed me. In all my years, I have heard about friends of mine getting head but for me I didn't want a wife of mine putting her mouth on me like that, but she is not my wife, girlfriend or anything. That first nut didn't take long and when it did come, she drunk all my nut. She sucked on my balls and licked me until I became exhausted with pleasure. I didn't want to go to sleep but we did. I would awake to her sucking on me. When she was tired of me lying down, she had me stand close to the wall. She knew what she was doing because after shooting a strong nut, I fell back on the wall as she kept drinking on me and teasing my balls. This time we took a nap.

When we woke up, she sat at the foot of the bed and let me jab her mouth for a while and when I nut, she sucked it slow and with ease. During this next session, the girl sat on the floor with her back to the bed and I buried my manhood in her face, but she was taking it like it wasn't anything to her. I tried to choke her, but she didn't let up. She took all of me including my balls in her mouth. You know I'm about well in length on hard; although, I heard her choke, but she continued on. She kept pulling and pulling until that nut came out in squirts. We went to sleep. Right before I woke up and came home to you, she smeared my nut all over her face, before drinking the rest out the stalk. She is a freak and one I would not care to see again. I tell you it's an experience I can't believe happened to me. This girl made me nut all night long, but it wasn't nothing like making love to you. I would rather been here making love to you."

My ears could not believe what they heard. I was angry because he is my husband, even if he abuses me. Marcus said, "You listening to me?"

"I just have a question."

"What's that?"

"Why didn't you let me be your first? You were my first in everything; even though we don't partake in oral sex?"

He looked at me and spoke, "One, we don't do that type of sex. Two, I don't want to kiss you or look at you and to think of the scandalous things you done to me in bed."

"Are you going to see her again?" I had to ask.

"No, that was just a one-time experience," he said honestly.

"What was her name?"

With a boyish grin he said, "All I know she said they call her Salty."

I didn't trust myself to talk. He said, "She did that, and you don't ever have to wonder about me asking you to do that because I would never. That part of my life is behind me."

We both sat there in silence. I didn't know what to say. He put his arms around me and said, "I can get up and cook if you want me too?"

"No that is ok. I can do it" truth be told I needed to be alone to process this information.

"Ok. Make it light."

I got up and went in the kitchen. I fixed an egg omelet with cheese and ham. I also put an orange in the middle with strawberries all around the orange. Putting the food on a plate, I placed the plate on the table. Going back in the bedroom, Marcus was about to take a shower. I stepped to the edge of the door and called out, "Your breakfast is ready."

He came out and looking as sexy as ever. I grinned and he moved the towel and twisted his hind parts and mumbled, "I take it you like it?"

"I do Mr. Grady. I really do."

He pulled me close to him and kissed me. Feeling aroused, I spoke, and "You better stop before things get out of hand."

"You sure you need me to stop?"

Shaking my head, no I stated back, "No not really."

I am learning not to let what he does get to me, even if it is horrific. I have to separate the good Marcus from the evil Marcus. Speaking nicely, "Mr. Grady, you're going to get me wet."

"Then I get to see you wet before I get you wetter."

He and I laughed as I began to disrobe my night gown. Marcus dropped the towel and waved for me to come on and we stepped back into the water. I followed him back into the water and closed the shower door. The water was drizzling down his masculine body and looping around the hairs on his chest. He took his hands and washed the water off his face to say, "You just going to stand there and watch or what?"

Taking the soap, he turned around and allowed me to wash his back, in small circles. He turned around and let the water wash the soap away. Marcus took the soap from me and started from on my back first. He lightly rubbed soap onto the sponge and caressed my back. Then he used the shower head and sprayed it off. I faced him. He kept his eyes on my breast as he touched them romantically. Using the sponge, he lathered it and affectionately took his time to wash each breast. His touch was driving me insane, and he knew it. He used the shower head and made the soap disappear by using an up and down formation. Marcus took his hand off the shower head and placed them all about me.

He rushed my breast with hot kisses. My arms wrapped around him instantly because they knew where they belong. My love did not say a word for words were not needed as he picked me up and sat me with ease upon him. For a few minutes he was taking me, and it was good. It seems like lately he has been having sex with me on a more personal level than ever. My husband has been messing with my mind and jacking up my senses mainly for the makeup sex and I'm getting in the routine of how he wants things done.

In my ear, my love was moaning and panting the words, give it to me. Just hearing his breathing in my ear was doing wonders to me. I have no idea where he found the strength, but he kept sticking it to me as he was drowning his crotch in me. My orgasm was causing me to pin his wet buttocks under me, while his orgasm was pinning me near the door wall of the shower. My legs flop as he finally let me go. I didn't think I could stand up when he released me, and I didn't. When the shower doors open, I fell out onto the floor. He was reaching for me, but he was too slow. I saw him standing at the door's edge laughing at me. I wanted to be mad, but it was funny. He stretched out his hand and said, "Here let me help you up."

"No. just leave me be. I'll get up," I spoke with humor.

Marcus laughed at me and helped me up anyway. I got up and dried off. I reminded him that I had cooked and how his breakfast was cold.

He replied, "We can warm it up or buy something else."

"I did cook for us."

"Ok, we will warm it up then."

We put on some lay around clothes and went in the kitchen. I warmed the food up as he waited. As I was opening the microwave door, he stated, "Child, I can't get enough of you."

"I can't get enough of you either."

"See if I was cheating there would be no way for me to yearn for the lovemaking you give."

Not really wanting to hear that, I removed those thoughts to say, "I am glad that is all out your system."

He sat down as I warmed up our breakfast. We ate and talked like a happily couple. It is times like this I love Marcus the most. He is being the man I married and not the monster that comes out in a full moon. We enjoyed the rest of our day with grace, even when my brother called, he was wonderful. I mean, he is always wonderful when my brother calls and talks to him, it is when my brother talks to me; that he has the problem.

For the next few days things were great. I have a tooth, and I have officially resigned as a highly qualified Math teacher. Marcus and I spent every waking moment together and it was bliss. We no longer argue and our love making is more explosive than ever. Even when his children call, he talked to them, and I always made sure I was busy so I couldn't. Although, when his grandchildren were on the phone, I would say hi and they would be nice back.

Marcus and I would play like children on a playground; especially hide and go get it. Meaning if whoever was it, had to find the person and if they found the person, they get to sleep with them wherever they were found. Sometimes, when I call out ready or not here, I come, Marcus would be lying in the middle of the floor naked. We would laugh as I proclaimed how he is not any fun. He would only reply that he was tired of making me wait so he gets right at it. The game was always fun. And at night, we would catch a movie or go out to eat, if we didn't want to dine in.

Nevertheless, I was getting my joy back. I felt like the Lord heard my cry about desiring to be happy because here I am happy as the day we got married. I didn't let his ex-wife bother me with her silly calls to him about their grown daughter not wanting to mind. On every occasion when he left the house, I was with him. We were doing more things together than we previously did. I had to keep calling him Mr. Grady because he said he liked the role playing. We didn't discuss the past; we left it there with hopes of our brighten future.

I felt pressure gripping my head as I tried to sleep. I turned over. Then I felt pressure on my shoulder. Finally waking up, it was Marcus. He gave that award winning smile and said, "I was getting your measurements and remembering where your joints are."

"For what?" I questioned.

"So, I will know how to chop you when I cut off your arms or to bust your head open. Pressure points are vital to know mainly if you don't want to do a lot of miss cutting."

I stared at him, and he snickered. I didn't find it funny. Marcus was carrying on like it was hilarious. I lay back down, and he wrapped his loving arms around me to place kisses on my neck creases. I pretended to be angry by saying, in a silly term to ease my uneasiness, "No get away from me."

"I can't leave you alone, even if I wanted too."

"And why is that?"

"Because of the emotions I have for you."

"Will you ever tell me you don't love me?"

"I will never tell you I don't love or want you. So, what does that tell you?"

I flipped around and asked, "Why is that? I mean if you are not in love then you aren't in love. I deserve the right to know if we are wasting time."

He got up and I learned to get up too. I sat in front of the mirror, and we stood getting dressed to reply, "Regardless what happens between us, I will always love you. I have been your first everything and do you know how rare you are? You are a precious jewel that I discovered for myself. I didn't uncover you for other men to like the shine you have."

"I was slow about relationships and sex because I was taught not to let every man put his sexual stick in your treasure. Other than that, I kept my head in the books. I wanted to be well off like my parents were so my children would not have to struggle."

"I agree. I guess that is one reason why Sharon, doesn't like my life with you."

The brushing of my hair came to a halt as I questioned with curiosity, "Why is that?"

"When we were married, we struggled a lot, but we managed. We couldn't do near bout the things that you and I can do."

"Like?"

"Eating out all the time, going on vacations, spending many nights at a hotel and materialistic things."

I started back brushing my hair as I said, "That is not how I am."

"You aren't but she is. She loves to shop and shop. She was spending more than I was making. Since I was the breadwinner, I have to pay her well over five hundred dollars a month in alimony until she gets sixty-two. I've already paid her two years' worth."

"Didn't you have that sent in already before we met?"

"Yeah, a judge sends it to her automatically. I paid the fifty-three thousand dollars upfront so her getting it is not on me."

Putting on my house shoes, I asked, "Isn't that steep? You have a new family, and all your children are grown."

"She took care of the girls when she could have worked. I didn't want her to work because girls need their mother at all times. I also needed my wife to not be tired if I needed her in any way. I supported her and her shopping habits. To be frank, that little money a month is not near enough for what she has done for me and the girls."

I made it by the nightstand and before I could question back from his reply, my cell played the fight song from my last job. I haven't heard that ring in a while and I was stunned to hear it now. Marcus picked up my phone to see who it was. I don't know how he got my new number, but he had it. Marcus's countenance fell so low I wasn't sure what to make out of it. He swiped the screen and put it on speaker. I spoke, "Hello."

"Hey there, how's it going on your end?"

It was Mr. Goss's voice, just what I needed. Trying to read Marcus, I stated, "Hold on a minute."

I touched the mute button to hear what Marcus had to say. He had anger on him as he asked, "What he doing calling you? You don't work at the school anymore and how did he get your number?"

"I don't know."

"You better check him because no man has the right to call my wife."

Taking the call off mute, I stated, "I'm back. How may I help you?"

"You crossed my mind, and I decided to give you a call. Haven't heard from you and I wanted to make sure you were doing ok. I asked Elisabeth about you, but she didn't comment so a friend of mine that worked at the phone company got your number for me."

Chapter 8

Marcus looked like he ate nails when Mr. Goss said I crossed his mind.

Right now, my heartbeat was thumping louder than the speaker. Marcus came closer to me to listen as if he would miss a secret code in the conversation. Not removing my husband out of my eyesight, I replied in haste, "Marcus and I are fine. Thank you for calling. I was in the middle of doing something and I have to go."

Ok. I want you to know that I think about the encouraging words you use to give me on our breaks. Those words helped me out more than you know and for that I thank you and hope you are happy. I want to encourage you this day to smile more and worry less."

My eyes never let Marcus out my sight. I spoke, "Your welcome, but I have to go now."

"Bye Mrs. Grady, take care."

"Bye Mr. Goss and you do the same."

My hanging up was not as fast enough. Marcus made my lips kiss my shoulder as I dropped the phone and fell against the wall. With my hand on my jaw, I glanced up at my husband. He clenched his mouth and stormed out the house. I cried out loud some. I haven't seen him like this in a while and now, since Mr. Goss called, I am in trouble. Pieces of me wanted to storm out behind him, while the rest of me stayed. I glanced out the window and saw how he jumped in the car and raced out the driveway. I began to pray, "Lord we were doing so well. Watch over him and keep him safe, Lord. He's angry again. Please watch over him. If I was wrong in any way forgive me and help me to do better by my husband. Amen."

I pulled myself together, picked up the cell phone and went down the hall to the living room. I made sure I had the phone beside me in case he called me. There was no way I was missing his phone call. I must be available at all times and can't be found complacent. My husband must see that I have always been dependable and understanding. After five hours of not hearing from Marcus, I took a chance and called. He answered. I sounded frantic when I said, "I was worried about you."

"I'm good. What you doing?"

"Sitting in the living room waiting to hear from you and now that I have, I'm better."

"I have a surprise for you."

"You do?"

"Yes. It's one of those surprises that will really surprise you. I want you to put curls all in your hair with those diamonds on those black open pins. I want you to be naked in our bedroom, so you won't mess your hair up."

"I'm excited already."

"Yeah, I had to get this for you so you can see just how serious love is."

"When you coming home with it?"

"I'll be home in a few but I want you in the bedroom, as I asked with the curtains closed; and no peeping."

"I won't peep, I promise."

"Good. I love when you promise me things and keep them. Goodbye."

I said goodbye as I hung up and did the things he asked of me. It was odd that he asked me to wear my hair like this. To be honest, I haven't worn my hair like that since our wedding. Wearing a smile like never before, I waited anxiously for him to come home with my surprise. About another two hours pass and still no Marcus. I was beginning to think he had forgotten about me. I thought I heard him in the yard. Not sure if I wanted to stand or sit, I decided to stand. I heard him pull up and I closed my eyes. I heard him calling out, "Child, where are you?"

"I'm in here," I yelled out to him.

He came in the room with a gorgeous yellow box that had a big red tie on the top. Handing it to me, he spoke with cheerfulness, "This is one of your surprises, Love."

Marcus handed me the box and in it was a magnificent light-yellow dress with deep crinkles of gold trimmings on a soft white hanger. The dress appeared expensive as it shined in the ordinary light. He demanded, "Let me see how it looks on you."

With shaking hands, I grinned in a happy speech, "It's remarkable. Where you get it?"

"I went shopping for you and when I saw it, I knew it was for you. Try it on while I go get your other surprise ready."

"Another surprise for me?" I spoke as I looked up at him.

"Yes, child, another surprise."

He left out and I put on the lavish dress. About twenty minutes later, he came back in the room and spoke, "You are truly beautiful in that dress. I knew you would be but to see it like this is so amazing to my eyes."

"Thank you for this dress. I look like a princess," I spoke as I did a twirl.

He smiled as he spoke, "You will always be my princess. You ready to see you other surprise?"

"I am!"

"Let me blind fold you."

"Blind fold? Ooh it must be really nice."

He took one of his long socks and tied it around my eyes. He guided me out of the bedroom to the living room. We came to a stop. He sounded happy when he said, "Take your time to open your eyes."

With my nerves all over me they housed eagerness and expectation of what was at hand. I removed the sock and streaked a little. I took my time to open my eyes fully. I assumed my eyes needed to readjust to the light, so I wiped my eyes and reopened them wider. It is here my mouth fell open and would not close. He screamed out, "Surprise!"

There before me on a roller cart was the most attractive yellow coffin I had ever seen. The gold flakes in the yellow color made the coffin sparkle like stars in a dark sky. It was truly a sight to see, and it is true that yellow is my favorite color, but I did not expect to find it like this. He opened the lid up. Inside was a white as snow with huge words, "Child I love you to death" inscribed in deep yellow in color.

Still my mouth was at a loss for words. I didn't expect this at all. He came over to me and held my hands with such an affection that caused me to still be at a loss for words. Pulling me closer to the casket, he said, "Isn't it a sight for your eyes?"

I could only shake my head yes. He went on to say, "I've searched all day for the most attractive eternal bed that money could buy."

Still my words could not form as he went on to say, "Look, I even have a golden pillow to rest your head on. It looks like you are sleeping in the heavens amongst the clouds, doesn't it?"

My eyes followed where he was talking about but still I could only nod. Marcus demanded as he sounded overjoyed, "Here feel. See how soft it is for you."

I did not reach my hands up. He plainly spur-of-the-moment put my hands on the soft white lining of the casket. I literally wanted to die from fear as he took my hands and made me squeeze the softness of it. Inside my mind, I was screaming and crying but dared not let it show. He opened it all the way up and showed me the rest of the white inside. He came and stood behind me as he wrapped his arms on me. Marcus acted like this was a regular gift a man gives his wife as he stated, "I know you are wondering why I bought you a coffin and that beautiful dress to match it?"

Shaking my head yes, he whispered in my ear, "Since you like to play with your life and mess with mine, I decided to show you where you will be sleeping forever because you won't be able to see it or appreciate it, when you're dead. I do these things because I love you and you don't understand how important you are to me, and you don't have a clue how important my vows are to you. I am an old man, and this Mr. Goss is a young lad. He will not enjoy you or the company you have ever. Take heed and replay back to this very moment at all you see. Be reminded what your future looks like when you decide to give him those encouraging words, Mrs. Grady."

Nothing came out my mouth as I tried to speak. He kissed me behind my hair and bumped my hair. Putting the spot back in place, Marcus continued to hold me with sincerity as he said, "No one will ever love you like I do. My old family is gone and all I have left is you and my love for you. There is no way I will let another man come in and sweet talk you. Not as long as I have breath in my body and if I don't have breath in my body, you won't either. That is a promise my dear and not a threat. You are my wife, and, in my day, we take vows seriously."

I continued to be without words. Marcus faced me and said, "I would never want to hurt you, but your loving drives a man like me to do stuff like this. I am intelligent and brilliant on other levels by that being said, not even Sharon made me do this to her. That is how I know my love for you is not on an equal playing field. It is unique and an original. Who would have thought that I would be acting like an irrational possessed man? I never thought that until you walked in my life. I had to have you although, Sharon and I were to reconcile our marriage, but I couldn't do it. You never purposely made me disillusioned about my family life or wife for that matter. Your innocence, your purity had my nose open and that was before I broke your virginity. I had to have you. You were all I could see and think. I could close my eyes and smell your perfume and when I opened them, I could see your beautiful smile. You got me going all over the place for you and that has never been done in my life. I know I love you. Can't you see you drive me out of my mind and that is why I do the crazy stuff I do? Talk to me."

He glared at me. The look in his eyes told me that he actually believed in the things he was saying to me. How can I not hurt him and live? I am casket sharp with a man that will make this a reality. Swallowing I said, "I am at a loss for words. I know you said you were bringing me a surprise home, I didn't think it would be this."

"I know Child, but you needed a surprise to make you think just how serious this love is."

Marcus walked over to the coffin, stretched his arms. He faced me to say, "Sometimes people have to see with their eyes and not abstract think of what it is. So, I make it plain for you to grasp and not go by what you believe. By doing this, I know we are on the same page and there is no room for either one of us to make a mistake about what the other one thought."

Letting his hands to fall to his side, he pointed to the casket and made his petition known, "After me this is the end for you. If you believe I am just trying to scare you; you are wrong. I will kill you and do me if I must. It won't be that one of us will make it, while the other one is dead; rest assure, if I do me- you already gone."

I tried to sound as warm as I could but had no luck when I asked, "Why are you so angry and bitter? I am not doing anything to jeopardize our marriage; my life for that matter."

He lifted his head to the sky and back towards me to say, "It's not that I am angry and bitter. You are mine and I must make you believe that."

Marcus raised his voice when he said, "And him calling you, calling you! Calling my wife!"

His chest began to rise and fall rapidly. He shook his head with rage because he could not finish the statement. His eyes became murky as I stood there frighten and unresponsive. He walked up on me and formed a wide letter C with his right hand. Sniffing as to not cry, he shook the letter while asking, "You see this?"

I agreed with my head, yes. He smashed the claw between my breasts and began digging his sharp nails into the thin fabric and my tender skin. My eyes widen as he said, "I will claw your heart out your chest and let you see it beat for the last time as you fall dead at my feet. Is that understood?"

My husband stood there poised and proud of the things he told me. He began to cry and cry as if I was the one beating on him. His conduct was that of a man thinking he's doing a great deed. Just his defensive actions, makes me cringe at the fact that I married him for love. His mere words sounded good to his own ears as the toxin from his mouth, touched me. From what I gathered, he is in love with the notion of loving me and not really loving me.

Marcus honestly believes his undying love for me is the best and how it is my fault he has done those things to me. Doing what I can to separate fantasy from reality caused me not to comprehend the madness my husband is telling me. Every vein in my body ran on its own for cover. My fight or flight instinct would not kick in, even with the danger in front of me. The thoughts in my brain would not think because they wanted no part of the lunacy that my ears and soul comprehended. Above all my tears watered up my eyes but that was all they did; for they too were also afraid to fall.

When I didn't say anything, he sniffled then dried up his face. Straightforwardly he demanded, "Get in the coffin."

That was too much as I stood there staring at him and the other half of the casket. I shook my head no because my words became silenced. In a loud frantic tone he said, "Get in the casket, Child and I will not tell you again."

I continued to shake my head no as I turned to take out running. Marcus came behind me and grabbed me to place my chin in his elbow. He had me in a sleeper hold. I fought as hard as I could to break free, but he was too strong. I could hear his harsh but scary voice encouraging me to sleep by saying, "Good night, Child. That's right; close your eyes and rest my Love."

The more I struggled the tighter the grip was on me and finally, I gave up. I don't know what happened next and I don't recall him saying anything else. I do remember waking up in a confined area. I already knew what it was I just didn't want to think what it was. Lifting my hands, I touched the top of the lid. It was cold, meaning the top hadn't been closed long. It was quiet, dark and had the smell of a new car. I began to let my tears go. They paraded down my face like a thousand float parade. I hit the ceiling of the coffin lid with the small space I had. I didn't want to rock the casket because I remembered it was sitting on a roller cart and importantly, I remembered that I have to remain calm for oxygen.

Silently, I pleaded, "Lord help me. Please God deliver me. Surely this is not my fate. You say you love me, and I have been praying for my marriage and my sanity, but you have not heard me. Please God hear me this day. I'm about to die, oh, God help me! I don't want to die like this!"

After that request, nothing happened. I waited about a few more seconds and still no answer. As if logic of smothering to death kicked in, I began freaking out and panicking. My breath was getting short as my head rocked to and from. Realizing just how confined the area really was hyperventilation was almost activated. Then I heard him almost yelling, "Be quiet and listen. If you do, I will let you out."

I didn't listen at first. He spoke it again, "Be quiet and listen and I will let you out."

This time, I became as quiet as I could. He said with a high pitch, "Remember if you are in there permanently there is no way out. For now, I hold the key and because I love you and I trust you, I will let you out."

Seconds later, the lid flew open, and I sprung upright, like a Jack in the box grasping for air. Marcus was there as I held onto him with all I had. He spoke nicely as ever, "Shush, I'm here; like always. I'm going to be the only one here for always. You hear me?"

As if I were a rag doll, Marcus helped me out the coffin. We held each other for a while. It's not that I wanted to hold him; I wanted to hold whoever was rescuing me from a fate worse than any. I trembled and trembled as words could not come out. All I could think about was how I was locked in a coffin, alive. Marcus pulled me from him to say, "I told you that I have your best interest, and I do. I am your protector, you hear me?"

The head on my body shook and shook yes as he said, "Come on Child, you need to change, and I need to let them come get the coffin."

He took me in the room and helped me out the dress. When the dress was off me, he had something in his hand as he stated, "Child, you must see this."

It was a picture of me in the casket. I looked so peaceful. I never thought I would see what I looked like in a coffin, but I am holding proof in my hands. He spoke as if he did a great deed, "I left the lid up the entire time you were knocked out. I am not as cruel as you may believe I am. When I got ready for you to wake up, I closed the lid and about one minute later, you woke up."

I was trying to stop crying as I listened to him and stared at the picture. He stood next to me as if I had a prize to say, "You look beautiful in that picture, if I do say so myself."

I didn't answer him. My husband got in front of me and shaped his hands like a V to put my face in it. He gazed into my eyes and right into my soul. I don't know what he was thinking but I was thinking, how I could love him and hate him at the same time? My crying never let up for I assumed, I was gone. Breaking my thoughts was his sensual tone, "I give you, my word. I will never do that to you again. So, love, please don't cry."

As much as I tried, I could not help it. From what I glimpsed, I slept all night and almost all evening in a casket. Although, I was out; that did not suffice me. Marcus took my cotton gown and wiped my tears. Now I am thinking he wants sex. I don't care to give him sex, but I know all too well what will happen if I fake or don't do it. My tears stopped as he wiped them away slowly. He smiled and spoke with softness, "That's better."

Trying to keep my wits, I could only reply, "Thank you."

"I can't lie, I want you, but I know you do not want me and for that I will wait for you."

That was a stunner. Lifting my head towards him I stated, "Thank you so much."

"Get some honest rest and I am sorry I did that. I was just painting a visual picture, nothing more."

Chapter 9

He left out and left me in the room alone. Thirty minutes later, a funeral home vehicle came and took the coffin away. He came back to give me a hug and a kiss. I didn't want his kiss nor touch but this evil thinking man has been the only man to arouse me. He just put me to sleep in a coffin but here I am in his arms like it never happened. What could be wrong with me? Maybe it is factual that he's broken me so far down that Jesus is the only one who can pick me up. Then my husband said, "Sarah rest and you can start back calling me Marcus."

I can start back calling him Marcus and not Mr. Grady, which, I am glad. Feeling better on that, Marcus turned the bed covers down for me and I crawled into them. I was not hungry, and food was the last thing I thought about. Closing my eyes was the easiest part; going to sleep was the hardest part. All in my sleep, I kept seeing that coffin and me in it. My thoughts rambled like never before. They were stating; what if he had buried me while I was sleep, what if I ran out of oxygen what could I had done if he took longer to let me out?

For weeks, I tried to make casual conversations in hope he would be the old him again. I even asked about his children because he sends them money all the time and he talk to them almost daily; nothing was working. Making do in this manner was not good enough. I still cried as my love did his best to cheer me up. It was like finding a safety place and not wanting to come out. I was safer in the house and Marcus was fine with that. I had him to park my car in the garage and leave it there. Being in the comfort of these walls was better for me. There have been times, when my own brother would come by, and I dared not to open the door for him.

I would silently watch him drive off from a far off, wishing I could leave with him. One time I almost stopped him but quickly changed my mind. I needed him to pray for me, but I needed to feel safe first. The more my brother would come, the more I ignored him. If I never opened the door when he came, then he must have gotten the hint that I wanted to live and not have any trouble come to me. A few more weeks passed, and I anticipated seeing my brother, but he never came back. I could not sneak and call because Marcus checks the phone records, and he has my calls forwarded to his phones. I can only call out and he better be the only one I was dialing. One day, my brother came with the police. Marcus had just gotten back from sending one of his kids some money as usual. I heard him say, "May I help you officers?"

"Does a Sarah White live here?"

"No, a Sarah White-Grady does. Who wants to know?"

"Sorry about that Sir but a Mr. Samuel White says you have his sister hostage and believes she is in danger."

Marcus let a hysterical laugh as if he heard a funny. The officer asked again, "Is she Sir?"

"Is she what?"

"In danger?"

"How is that?"

"Mr. Grady, we request that his sister comes to the door."

"You come to my door asking for my wife."

"Sir we understand how this may sound but we have to check on every call or on any persons that is believed to be in danger. Again, we request that his sister comes to the door."

Marcus closed the door and came to me. I pretended that I didn't know what was going on. He got in my face and said, "Your stupid brother thinks I am holding you hostage."

"How is that when you are my husband?"

"Go to the door. Handle that and get back in this house. Don't be out there long."

"I won't."

Putting on my house shoes, I came to the door. Sam rushed me hurriedly and said, "I know he is stopping you from seeing me. I am your brother Sarah."

"He is not stopping me from seeing you. I just don't want any company."

153

"What is he doing to you? Has he threatened you? Is he beating you? What is he doing to you?"

Glancing back at the door, I pleaded, "Sam please leave it alone."

My brother saw the urgency in my tone and said, "What has he done to you? You don't look the same anymore. I barely recognize you. I am your brother, and I know you are terrified. Let me help you. Please let me help you. My sister you are the only immediate family I have here. I don't want to lose you."

I stopped my brother to say, "Sam you see that I am well, just go away and keep me in prayers. Do that for me. Believe God now, more than ever."

He turned to the officers and asked, "What can you do?"

"Sir, she has not given us a reason to think there is a problem."

Marcus came to the door and was rude when he said, "You all need to get off my property and go find a doughnut shop."

The officers standing by us turned to Sam and said, "Sir you see she is fine, and we must vacate the premises."

Sam took a sigh and gave me a final hug. Marcus stood there watching me and my body language for whatever out of the ordinary. My brother turned to Marcus and said, "If my sister comes up hurt or missing, you will answer to me."

Giving my brother a sly smile, he said, "Officers don't you hear him threaten me?"

The police were quiet. The tall one spoke, "Sir we heard no such thing."

"Leave now!" Marcus yelled.

I went back inside as they all left. He came to me and said, "You handled that very well."

"Thank you love, I mean Marcus."

While he went back to bed, it occurred to me that he is all I have. My brother and I don't see one another, I don't have a job because Marcus take care of me, I had friends but that was a long time ago and now my life is centered around pleasing Marcus and how to make him happy. With that thought, I went to be bed and lay beside him. A few hours later, I heard Click, click.

I peeped out and saw I was still in my dark and cozy room. Again, I couldn't make out what it was then I heard it again, click, click from behind me. This time I rolled over and in my face was silver instrument. My brain recognized that it was a gun. I jumped up hiding beside the bed, screaming, "Don't shoot! Don't shoot!"

Then I heard the laughter. It was Marcus as he said, "Love I was playing Russian roulette with you."

I believed I used the bathroom on myself as I ran to the toilet. In my background, Marcus laughed at me. I was nervous and afraid to do anything. He could have shot me, I thought. My husband spoke in a cruel manner, "Come on. The gun doesn't have but seven shots and you were on number four."

Each time I tried to get up, my bowels would not stop running, which caused me to sit down rapidly. He literally scared the shit out of me. My nerves were out of whack as I could hear the clicking of the gun in my ears. He came to the door and said, "I thought you would have woken up on the first two, but it took you two more clicks. Love you can't be sleeping that hard, when you in the bed with me."

He closed the door for he was right. Silently I sat on the toilet and said, "Lord this is no way for me to live. Why won't you hear me! Please God do something. I can't keep living in this madness. You have to do something before I do something."

I wiped myself, flushed the toilet and washed my hands. I stared in the mirror and still no answer from Jesus. I turned to walk away but stopped. It hit me. This is the first time I have truly looked at me in a mirror in months. I mean really looked at me. Not when I had on the yellow dress but to gawk at oneself. My skin had a dull appeal to it. I've become very thin. It's not that I was big, but I can tell that I have lost every bit of fifty pounds. The sight of me was hideous. I've let myself go for fear and if I look like I use to, Marcus would think that a man wants me.

However, it is easier this way. I can go unseen and undetected. If I am not attracting attention that I won't have a problem; then again this is Marcus. I finally saw him standing in the mirror behind me. He said with such displeasure, "Yes, you look horrible. Can't you fix yourself up, Sarah? You are a woman, and I am a man that still has eyes."

I didn't say a word. I jumped when he yelled, "Are you deaf? You don't know how to look good for me anymore?"

Soon as I could speak, I said, "I do. I just don't know how you will take it, Marcus."

"I take it that you can't keep my attention at home, and you need some help."

Retaliating, I retorted angrier, "I think I'm already getting it."

"You think you getting it?"

Being sterner in my words, I said it louder, "I believe you already seeing someone because you always come home humming."

"Maybe you don't turn me on or can't keep me turned on. Your breasts are sagging, and you aren't even old."

When he spoke that, I glanced at my breast. He then said, "You have a fake tooth, your buttocks are disappearing and only God know your sex is useless, but I still work it because I love you."

Getting upset, I retorted bitterly, "If I am like that, stop torturing me and torture someone else. I have a fake tooth because you snapped, remember?"

Being Marcus he stated, "Why torture someone else, when I can torture you; my wife?"

He closed the bathroom door and turned off the light. I heard the same familiar click as he called out, "Number one."

"What sick mind game are you playing now because I want to go back to sleep?" I asked.

"It's called if you don't move the right way you will get shot."

"Go somewhere else and play, I am not in the mood."

Words were not formed but I heard the spinning of the bullets. It clicked as he said, "I have a bullet in here and I am pointing where I think you may be hiding. If you hit me, I will shoot you on purpose. Understand?"

"Marcus," I said as my heart was racing in my ears.

Our bathroom is big but not big enough to have a lot of things to hide behind. The click was heard again as he yelled out, "Number two."

Panic set in. I looked around for somewhere to hide but making sure I was not near him. Something told me to lie on the floor in front of the mirror. To see if he was really pointing at me, I reached up and threw my perfume by the toilet. I heard the click point that way. He is really trying to shoot me, I thought. When he said number three, I heard the gun go off. He flicked on the light. We both saw that he shot out the bathroom window, which was about two feet from where I previously was. I was scared. I cried as he said with disappointment, "You cry too much with these games. Now I have to change ammo."

He left out. I am a nervous wreck and scared for my life. I could hear him in the bed. Marcus then screamed back at me, "Come on to bed, I need some of that good pussy."

I continued to lay there in dismay. Quietly I asked the Lord, "How can I perform after going through this? Help me; please God to act in such a way that he would not know how I am truly feeling. Amen."

Marcus yelled, "You taking too long!"

I pulled myself together and walked out the bathroom taking off my clothes. I have to put on a performance even if it kills me. He lifted his head up to say, "That's what I'm talking about."

He lay back on the bed as I climb towards him saying, "I want to give you what Salty been giving you."

"I don't know if I want a wife of mine performing such an act."

"Why not?"

"I have to look at you in the morning and all I may be able to see is what you did to me last night. That may spoil it for me."

"We can try it once and if it spoils it for you than I won't attempt it again."

I had my hand stroking his shaft with passion. He liked the feel for it was getting longer in my palm. He asked me as to encourage me, "You sure you want to try it?"

"Yes. You are the man I love and why not experience this on you?"

He was silent some more before saying, "Her mouth can melt a ten-pound bag of ice cubes."

"She may melt ice cubes; I'm melting ice blocks."

Marcus let out a sexual sound or arousal. Moving his legs back and forth he spoke with ease, "There it is. Drink it."

Not sure what to do, I played back how he said she did it. I put my butt towards him so he can play in my vagina, like he did Salty. Going slow like I remembered, I began pleasing my husband. On a few instances he would hold my head, and I would choke. The entire time I prayed it didn't take long because I didn't like it and don't see how Salty likes it. Timing could not have been better. Soon as I came up off him, his semen spilled out the little hole at the top of his stick. I was at awe about it for I have never seen such a sight, not even in a movie. Marcus looked at me and stated, "I don't want you to ever do that again."

"Was I that bad?"

He was quiet before saying, "No but it is ruined."

"What is?"

"Never mind, go and scrub your mouth out and don't talk to me."

I thought I was doing it the way he likes but I was not. He said it was ruined. I am thinking the tasting Salty does to him was better than mine and

163

it should be. She is more likely a pro in that area; where he was my first. Turning on the water, and getting my material, I began to scrub my mouth and lips just like he commanded me to do. Staying in the bathroom a long time, I was making sure my mouth was clean, and it was. I came out and Marcus was gone. I sighed and don't know if it was of relief he was gone or relief that I don't have to face him. Either way, my husband was gone. I got in bed and went to sleep.

I didn't want to think of Marcus or the act I performed. I didn't want to think of me in that coffin or anything he had done to me. I wanted to sleep without thinking of anything. The next day, Marcus was happier with me in this state of being, but I wasn't. I know when he's visiting Salty because he would always come home humming a tune. Plus, he would stay out all night and I would pretend to be sleep when he eased into bed. He had no idea that I hadn't been sleeping either. This hostile environment had me up when he was up and sleeps when he was sleep; this way I knew his movement. Here come the tears all over again. I tossed and turned for a long time and sleep never put me in dream world. I got up and stared out the window.

Altogether my life before my husband was joyous. My temperament was happy, and my character was that of one who loved life and the people in my life. I wasn't afraid to answer my phone, and I wasn't afraid of death until now. I am just now seeing that I've lost weight, a tooth, pride and dignity. I've lost my self-esteem, my hope, my voice, my way of thinking, my faith in God and own identity. It's funny how it took twenty-six years to wait on the right man and still feel the one you with is wrong. I called myself taking my time to better myself, in this way when I met Mr. Right, I would know him. He would not be one given in to drink or smokes. He would be compassionate, kind, considerate, caring and hopefully one of faith.

On top of that he would, be thankful to have me, a virgin that has saved herself just for him. It is not about being pure but doing right. I had imagined the man I love would be honest to me and that I would be all he needed in a wife, friend and lover. How could I have lost my focus? I am

165

nowhere like I used to be, and I am nowhere the person I wanted to be. In all my day, I would not have thought to be in a marriage; nevertheless, in a relationship like I am in now. Some reason known to man; I am drawn to my husband like milk from a cow. I got it in my mind that, if I don't see it, then it didn't happen.

I found myself making up excuses for his way of teaching me life. However, I love math and one plus one is still two but not anymore. I've added other numbers but the main number I see is the two; that is Marcus and me. He has shot in the room where I was standing, changed my name and yet; I love him. When I am not on the phone with him, I better be sleep and yet; I love him. He has divided me from my only family and yet; I love him. Marcus is the Ring Master that tells me, the animal what to do and I do it. He shakes his whip, which is his fist, and I come running.

If he tells me to jump off a bridge, I'm asking which one? How did all this come about? How did this type of love and living enter my life? When did I lose myself and found a new self? Shaking my head, I wiped the tear that fell.

This isn't the type of love I imagined all those years ago. This isn't even the type of love my parents had for one another and yet; I am in it. My dad had never hit my mom or verbally abused her to my knowledge and here I am getting hit on in the dark and waking up to the clicking sound of a gun. My tears found a way out of my eyes and this time, came down my face.

At those words, I glanced at my arm and glad that it is healed. This scare is the only physical scare anyone can see. What about the ones' they can't see? What about the emotional and psychological scares that may not ever leave me as they plague my every moment? What about the knots in my head that my hair covers? What about being afraid to sleep when he is at home? What about all of that? I call myself talking to Jesus, but he has not heard me. I am alive but dead to how things should be and yet, no answered prayers. I have cried out to the Lord and still this man of mine, do these inhumane acts to me. The Word tells me to not faint and in due season I would be rewarded.

Where is my due season? Where is my reward for trying to be faithful to HIS Word? I can't even hold my head up high anymore. I don't even attend church and I know I am not to forsake it, but I have although, his children and ex-wife are not there to bother me, I just don't think I can pretend in the presence of Holy Ghost filled people that may or may not understand my life or the things I have been going through. I am alone in this world, in this house for that matter while my husband has visitations with another woman.

Where is the love in that? I thought more as I cried harder. I desire to leave but each single time I make up my mind too, he comes home, or we start back being "the us" that got me the way I am now. All I have is Marcus. All I do is for Marcus and all I plan to accomplish will be with Marcus unless a miraculous thing happens in my life to turn this around. The more I sat at this window, the more I thought about my love for my husband. How could one so bad be so good? How can you not want sugar, if your body needs it for insulin? You can't. Sugar is as vile to your body as calcium is to your bones. That is how it is with my love. I didn't plan on it being like this, but it is.

Suddenly the headlights from his car were full force. I saw time had gotten away from me as I jumped back into bed. Now is not the time for my nerves to have their own mind. I did everything to stop from shaking because he spooks me. What if he saw me? My mind said loudly, which made me shake harder. I heard him come in the house and I heard the door lock. I heard him coming down the hall because the bedroom door was the same way he left it.

Chapter 10

"Wake up Love, I'm in need."

Marcus pulled off his clothes and got in the bed. He reaped of strong liquor. Pretending to have been awakened by him, I asked slowly to allow him to see me turn my nose up. I stated, "You been drinking again?"

"I went to the bar and had a few shots of gin. Then I started thinking about your soft skin and pussy. Now shut up and give me what I've asked for."

I touched him below and he was already ready. I began to think that he has previously been tasted by Salty or whoever because he is rock hard. I threw my gown on the floor so I could proceed with the foreplay, but he said, "I don't need the foreplay right now, love. I need to get between your legs."

"How you want it?"

"The way I love."

I got in the middle of the bed on my back. Before he climbed on top he said, "I need you to hold me in tight. I'm in the mood to go deeper than ever."

That stirred me. No matter how bad things are between us, the sex is always fantastic. It makes me want nothing else when I am lying in this bed. I don't think of things. I only think of pleasing Marcus. He stared down at me in a rare manner. He spoke as if he really meant it, "I am blessed to come home to you and your love. I have never stopped loving you and I take pride when I make love to you."

He bowed his head and placed them between my breasts. He was kissing them and smelling them. He moved his head to and from, between them like a man that could not get enough. The very contact of his lips on them stirred me while his kisses taunted me. Utilizing what I had, I buried his head in the small mounds. Knowing what I like, his tongue played with the erected nipples for fun. Moans of desire spit from my mouth. He said he didn't want foreplay, but he is giving it to me. Removing his head and lifted up.

This is the part that melts away and clears my mind. It is here that he enters me with perfection. Momentarily he stared into my eyes while his manhood was at attention in me. In an almost cry, he spoke unclearly "I had to pause because this is too much for me."

He didn't give me a chance to speak. Marcus began moving like a wave on top of me and I was rippling back to him. He went from side to side and circles as while going slow. We have gone slowly before but to be at this level was not really us. My husband was acting like there was nothing in the world but us. To be truthful, there isn't. Who is to disturb us? Who is to call or come by to see us? No one; therefore, he can take his time to stay up there as long as he like.

But the speed increased. He was no longer going slow but making his body dance on top of me. I opened my eyes and saw how his eyes were closed and sweat was dripping all about him. I could barely hear him as he mumbled, "Good, good, good, good."

With each time he spoke the word good, he was down pumping inside me with pressure. Marcus was not letting up on me for one minute. I am surprised that I have room to move because he usually pins me to the bed, and I can't throw it back like I want until he gets ready to climax. However, he began to speed grind me. My legs were sweaty and from time to time they would drop off his hips. But as superior as it is I would put my legs back into position. When that didn't work, I would take each hand and hold each ankle. I was keeping my pose just for him to continue the massive dick throwing he was doing. Then my lower half, agreed with my mouth, "It's good. I can't take it, can't take it."

"You are doing a good job to me!"

Hearing that alone caused my orgasm to rupture strongly and boldly. My moans were soft as I cried, then Marcus screamed silently as he froze. It is here when he stays hung inside of me. I didn't want to let my legs drop because of the thumping I could feel from the pin hole of his love jabber. Marcus peeped out his eyes and shook his head causing some of his sweat to fall

173

upon me. He started easing out of me in a slow drag. This allowed me, to feel him removing himself from me. It was like my vagina was begging for him to come back. But the get right tool slipped on out.

Truth be told, I felt sadden because it wasn't in me anymore; although, it is beside me. It seems the only way he isn't doing harmful things to me, is when he was making love to me. I scooted up and lifted up so he could put a pillow slip on the wet spot. Marcus got back on his side and said, "Love, no matter what I say or how I act, your loving is the best and I can't leave it alone. I admit I do not do all the way right by you, but I have to have you all to myself. I don't want to share you or your body with anyone. Is that selfish?"

"It's not selfish, if that is what you like," I spoke to agree with him.

"It is not what I like. It's what I love and sex with Sharon, wait can I say it?"

"Yes. She is your past while I am your future. Go on and tell me."

Marcus pulled me closer and spoke, "Sex with Sharon has never in all our years been this explosive. I mean, even if I have you in a position where you can't move, it's good and when I give you a little space to move, it is even better."

"Really?"

"I have had my share of sex but yours is the "to die for piece" that I will kill for. It's not just the sex. It is you as an individual and I have told you this before."

"You have."

"You don't have to do nothing to me. What I'm saying is like mess around or things of that magnitude. You don't have to do any of that for me to want to kill you. I can't share you, not even with a baby."

"A baby?"

"Not even with a baby."

"Have you forgotten we did lose a baby?"

"I haven't forgotten. I am not glad that we lost a child, but it is a part of us but right now we don't have any and I don't want any."

"You don't?"

"I thought I did but when that one got away and our lovemaking has been so intense there is no way, I want to share you with a baby."

"A baby is a baby, and I hope to have one or two one day."

"As of right now, no baby in our future."

"Why?"

"You going to think this silly, but I have been thinking about this for a while now."

"Ok, I'm listening."

"If you got pregnant, I would have to share your beautiful breasts."

Being careful not to laugh, I stated, "They are breasts that will house milk for the baby."

"When you're pregnant, your breast will grow and become sore, am I right?"

"That is the purpose."

"If they stay sore all the time, you wouldn't want me to taste them at will. I won't be able to make you moan as you do when I put them each in my mouth or tease the nipples because of the milk forming."

"Good point but still."

"Wait I am not finish."

"There's more?"

"If you are pregnant, the baby will have a house in your uterus for nine months, correct?"

"Yes, that is where a baby normally lives in a mother to be."

"If the chap is in there my manhood can't be."

"What?"

"You heard me."

"Your manhood will not reach to my uterus."

"The only thing I want inside of you is my dick. It'll be in your best interest if you don't get pregnant."

I glared at him and saw how serious he was. How can he be serious about me not having a baby, so I asked, "You really don't want your baby inside of me, do you?"

He brushed his finger lightly to my cheek and responded, "Children are greedy and will drain you dry. They only want to take and take. We don't need that. You don't need that. Look at mine?"

"Those are yours and Sharon's. I want one of our own."

"Not now. You are young and who knows. I don't want to talk about it."

Marcus turned over and we went to sleep. The things he told me was ridiculous, but I better not say that to him. A few hours later, I got up and went to the bathroom to shower. Before stepping out the shower, I reached for the towel and my hand was hit. I wiped the water off my face and saw Marcus. He stood there with a long thorny switch. Acting like a parent about to chastise a child he said, "You have a silly notion of having children but not today."

He drew back and in full swing he let loose. The contact of the switch to my skin was horrible.

I was yelling at him to stop but he wouldn't. He was saying, "Didn't I tell you no baby! Get that idea out your head right now!"

All I could do was to agree and holler. In every place he hit me I would reach for that area like I was stopping him. I slipped onto the floor, and he lashed out on me harder and harder; all I could do was cry out. He was chastising me like parents do a tender child that disobeyed. The whipping occurred over two or three minutes. When he finished with me, I assumed he went back to sleep. I got out crying inside my mouth, to make sure he did not hear me. I finally got up and saw the blood trail markings all over my legs, thighs, and arms. I know for sure on my back for I can feel them.

This is becoming too much for me. I have been praying and seeking God and I feel that I am doing it in vain. With nowhere to go, and no one to turn too, I immediately spoke through tears "Jesus, how could you allow this to happen? How could you let him do this to me if you so called love me! What have I done to receive such treatment? Why won't you answer me! If I have been wrong and sinned against you, please forgive me! I can't think of anything in my life that constitutes for the way I have been treated. I was always good to my parents. I have always done what was right but how is it that I am being abused by my husband, my lover and feeling abandoned by you? I try oh God, how I try to be a wife. Oh God how I try to be a woman to the man you have given me. Since his retirement, he has done nothing but rough me up and yet he goes unpunished. I still pray for him, even when I don't want too. Someway my husband makes me love him and yet, he makes me detest him so. How is that God! How is it that he does what he does, and I pretend that it is all ok? Is this the type of life you want for your child! Is this the way I am to live all my life! God, why you won't answer my prayers? You act like you don't see my tears or hear my cries. What am I to do, that I may get your attention? You haven't saved me from this pain that I am experiencing; so, what am I to believe? I've done my best to keep your commandments, paid tithes, counseled those in need to lead them to you; and yet I am in need of deliverance and no avail."

I believe I have cried out. My God says he won't forsake me and here I am mad at HIM for not helping me. I continued to think about my life. I thought about what ifs and could have been. Then reality hit me, that I am married to a monster and that I am angry at God for not delivering me. I am not getting it. For weeks at a time, he would be the wonderful man I married then he would change into a creature straight out of Hell. I just don't get it. Regardless of how it looks, I still prayed to the Lord Jesus for strength and yet; my life is not much better.

The next few days were bad for me. I could not sit down and lying down on my back was almost impossible. I greased the blisters and stayed out of his way. When he would come in the house, I would be asleep and while he was there, I stayed in the room. He didn't ask me to cook or anything. I would go to bed then he would come in and each time he turned, I turned and peeped to make sure he was still in bed asleep. This was getting to me, and I feel a break down is on the way.

On this day, he came in the house quickly. I heard him call for me, but I had just got out the tub, as fast as I could, I grabbed my robe before he has a chance to snap again. Putting it on, I rushed out the room and into the kitchen, out of breath and screaming, "You called?"

He stared then spoke, "Sit here for a minute."

I sat down at the table, and he said, "I think you should know why I whipped you a few days ago."

What do I say? I thought as I said nothing. He then continued, "I wanted to kill that seed before it had time to take root. I don't want you to let the notion of having kids get in and before I know it, I'm in on the plan. I've already had a reversal and wished I hadn't done that but anyway that is all I had to tell you."

"Okay," was all I could say.

"You mad?"

Wanting to tell the truth but decided to only say, "You whipped me with a switch like I am a child."

"Technically I am old enough to be your father."

"But you are not him," I said in a nice tone.

"Then you should not have acted like a child and thought like a wife who respects her husband's wishes."

Marcus got up and brought a plate back. It was some warmed-up tacos. He said, "Here. I know you haven't been eating and if I want you a certain way then I must do what I must to get you a certain way."

"What way is that?"

"Submissive."

"I'm not submissive?"

"You are to a degree."

"Then what are you talking about? I have done nothing but show love to you and yet you traumatize me beyond my wildest dreams."

Sternly he spoke, "Just like that day I told you no baby and you being young and family orientated you want children. I know it's not your fault that I have four already and you don't. Now if you had that one my ideology might have changed but personally, I don't want us to have any children."

"I hadn't thought of any children until you brought it to my attention."

"What? You don't want children by me?" He spoke furiously.

Quickly to right any wrong, I said, "I do but since all this way of showing me love has been going on, no. I don't want to bring a child into the world."

"Good answer."

Chapter 11

His cell phone rung and I already knew who it was; one of his needy children. He got up and went outside. I want to hear what they are saying but I know he has things in a certain order that only he knows how it is. Deciding to just sit there and do nothing. What can I do? If it hadn't been for Marcus, I would have nothing. I don't have a job, but I do have the money from my parent's death. Marcus came back in and said, "Marianne needs some money before they turn her lights off."

I did not say a word. He spoke a little louder, "You hear me?"

"I do."

"Well?"

"You want the truth?"

"Yes please."

"Elisabeth is the only child you have that doesn't ask for your money. The rest believe because you are daddy, your job is to take care of them, and you do. They need a husband to help them with their needs and stop depending on you when they are in need. I understand helping your children but to jump all the times they need this and that. Just because you have money does not mean you want to spend it on them. If they still want to be taken care of like a child, then they should have never moved out into the real world. By you doing all these things for them what about us or what about if I need things too and you can't give it to them because we in a need? Although, we have money but if you keep giving it to them, you won't have it to give; then who's going to help you? Surely not me because I don't have a job and nor do I have friends that I can go to if I needed things."

He beheld my face as my words-soaked in. I don't know why I told him all that, but I did. Normally he would get me for saying stuff against his children but what more can he do to me, than he already has done. Shaking his head to agree with me, I heard the words, "You right."

My mouth fell open as I heard him say that. It has been so long and to have him say that made me feel like I have made a huge accomplishment.

Using surprise as my crutch, I questioned, "You serious?"

"Yes. There are not many times they call me just to check on me. A lot of occasions they need gas money for work, pay a rent, grocery or things for my grandchildren. Marianne doesn't ask for much like Tonya and Katie so what do you think?"

"Sharon can't help them. She is their mother and one they listen to."

"She is selfish and can be uncaring but if they really need it, she will do it."

"They are her children and your children, all the same."

"You never had to tote water or eat bologna and hot dogs just to make it. We have. You don't know the feeling of living in a rundown home and hope if company comes over, they won't go to the bathroom because the plumbing isn't working, you can only imagine how it is to empty a piss bucket or have a warm room and a cold bathroom, living room and kitchen. You never had two sockets working in the entire house and have to unplug this or that to cook?"

"You right."

"I've been through a lot of that with Sharon and the girls. I can only guess that is why I help them as much as much as I do."

"I understand."

"I know they are grown; I wish I could have had a better job to take care of them while they were young. That goes back to when the pastor said we spoil our children because we don't want them to come up as we did but the way we came up did not kill us and for that we handicap our little blessings in a way. I bet the first thing she hollers is, go tell your daddy or get it from your daddy I don't have a job."

"Why would she say that?"

"Because I have money and plenty of it. She also knows I will bend over backwards for my loves."

"But still, that isn't any reason to suck you dry with a straw."

He and I laughed. I asked, "How much is her bill?"

"Eighty dollars."

"Go on and send it but get on the phone with the rest of your girls and let them know you are not the money dispenser or a financial bank for them like that."

"Ok. I will do that."

Marcus called Marianne and had her to put them on three-way calls. He told them no more money unless it is very important and how he is not going to help them out as much. They threw me up of course but he was nice about it and defended me. The oldest did a temper tantrum but that did not work with Marcus. This is so surreal. I must be dreaming; I thought as he told the goodbye. Not believing what I heard, I spoke with surprise, "You really took up for me!"

"Yes."

I ran and hugged him as tightly as I could. I kissed him on the jaw and gave him a squeeze. This is the first time in a long time, I actually feel like smiling and feeling confident that things are about to be better for me. He said, "I did it because you my wife and I saw how you turned Sam away. Surely if you can turn away your only brother, surely, I can stop being a money machine for my grown daughters."

Giving him a real smile, I voiced loudly and proudly, "The Lord answers prayers."

"What prayers have you been sending up? I hope it was about me."

"I always pray for you and our marriage."

"Love don't give up praying for me. I am undone and unlearned in many areas that the Lord has to work on, but he is not finished."

"You don't have to worry about that."

Wiggling his fingers for me to come to him, I did as if I was a puppet on a string. Marcus led me to sit upon his lap and I did. Placing my arms about his neck, I said with love, "Mr. Grady, it's been a while since you had me like this."

"It's been too long. But I tell you what. Let me throw these old ass tacos out and take you to a nontraditional Thanksgiving dinner and make up shopping."

Sounding happily, I stated, "Mr. Grady I would love that immensely."

"We can go to those side malls and hold hands before you pack my arms full of bags."

"Sounds like a plan to me."

"Let me freshen up and put on some plain clothes."

"Ok."

I jumped up and changed into a nice jogging set. I made it back to the kitchen and Marcus was waiting on me. He smiled that warm smile and said with love, "You are beautiful and I'm not sure I want you out in the public eye."

"They can want all they want. I know who it is that has my heart and my body."

"We might postpone and have a little more fun."

"We have all night."

"You right. You drive going, Love, and I drive back."

Seductively I stated, "I love it when you drive."

Marcus gave my butt a spank as we walked out and got in the car. The first place I went to was J. C. Penny's. I haven't been in a shop like that in a long time and it was strange to be out in public and looking at things with Marcus. I spent almost four hundred dollars quickly and Marcus didn't exchange a word. He was as excited as I was. I wanted him to pick out clothes that he would love to see me in. He told me I already have my birthday suit and that is the one he will pay any day to see.

We laughed about that as we took a break at Ruby Tuesday's. I don't know where I got this cheap mentality from but all during today, I noticed how cheap my taste had become. It's not that I buy expensive things but with the stuff I had been going through, I have to have him nearby to make sure my clothes are wife appropriate, and they were. It took us about an hour in the restaurant before leaving to another store. This time I told him I want him to get something for himself. He picked out the Big and Tall store.

I haven't been in there in a long time and was unsure about going but he told me that I made him go in that woman's store. I parked the car, and we went inside. It wasn't packed which I like because a big crowd is to some degree is what I don't need. It's almost Thanksgiving and there is so much I want to do but I know it won't happen. Forgetting about the approaching holiday, I began picking out Marcus some nice winter clothes.

He has suits but not many clothes to relax in or clothes just to lounge around the house, other than his pajamas. We weren't there ten minutes when the guy asked us for help. Marcus went to try on a pair of joggers. When he came out the guy and I both told him they fit him perfectly. The helper and I talked a little more as Marcus tried on more pants. We were standing earshot of his dressing room so he could hear everything being said. My love came back out the dressing room asking what I thought about the army outfit he had chosen.

I didn't really like it because if I am learning him like I believe I am, all the things he does has a point behind it. That is why I have to be careful of what I say and how I say things. He does not forget. In part, I want to boost him to go back to work, with hopes he would stop being so mean to me, but I will discuss that later. Marcus finally came out and asked the helper, "Is she the "to die" for?"

I was stunned. An odd feeling came over me as the helper questioned, "Excuse me, Sir?"

I turned away from them to walk off, but Marcus grabbed me by the arm and spoke, "Whoa where you think you going, Ms. Talkative to single men?"

I felt humiliated. If I could have melted through the floor and out the door, I would have but leaving was not going to happen. Marcus stated back to the helper with bitter, "I asked you if she is the "to die" for?"

"Sir I don't understand your question."

"How about this? I hope she is the "to die for," because she is the "to kill" for."

The young guy who appeared to be around his early twenties took a few minutes to understand what was spoken; once he understood it, he stepped to my husband with confidence. Having a level head, he stated to Marcus, "Sir we just standing here where you can hear. It's not like that but we can make it like that. The same way I found this job, I can find another one."

Getting between the men, I said, "Come on it's not worth it."

"Yeah, take your daddy home before he gets stomped in this store."

I turned to look at the young man, and then very quickly, Marcus came around me and chopped the young man in the throat. The helper grabbed his throat as Marcus began punching him like it was nothing. I tried to stop it as a cashier came over to help stop the attack. The young man was on the floor when we finally got Marcus off him. The manager yelled, "Call the police."

"I'm not going anywhere. Let them come! They can get some too."

"Come on baby, let's go. Let's go. Marcus let's go," I begged and pleaded for him to come on.

The manager stated, "You better leave, Mr."

"What? You want some," Marcus stated to the manager that came to assist the injured worker.

"Leave my store."

"You tell that young punk to leave my wife alone and don't say another word to her!"

About the time we walked out the store, we saw the police. I thought the manager was going to report us, but he didn't. I think he was just as afraid as I was. Marcus got in the car and drove off. At first, I didn't know if I should say anything, but he spoke as if nothing happened, "I wasn't going to let that young punk disrespect me like that, especially in front of my wife."

"Marcus, it wasn't like that."

"He had no business even talking to you."

"You were standing right there while we were talking."

"It doesn't matter where I was if he is all in your face, does it?"

I glared at him and spoke very defensively, "He was not in my face like that. He was just talking about clothes for men."

"Then he should have been talking to me and not you, then."

"He only asked what kind of style you were looking for and what was the amount you wanted to spend. I told him we were not caring about the amount; we only wanted some nice clothes. He said well this store was high, but the clothing is of good quality. Then he asked what your style is. I told him that we live in the country, but you don't have a style per say but we were looking to find you one. Then you came out and went back in. I said as long as it is not stripes and polka dots he laughed and so did I. That was it."

"I know I was in there listening."

I stated, "Then why come unglued, if you heard it all?"

"Young punks these days want women like you. They get you talking and carrying on. Before I know it, you sleeping with him and left me."

"It will take more than a conversation about clothes to get me to leave the man I love."

"I couldn't tell. You were laughing like he was a comedian."

"What you mean by that?"

"Young women are not only young, but they can be just as dumb if they don't have the right man; they would mess up. Fortunately, you have the right man to keep you in check. You don't see it but if you nice to them, they think they can come in and have you. They can't have what belongs to me; not in this lifetime or the one to come."

"It wasn't like that at all. You are making something out of nothing."

"You were just laughing away and carrying on you would not have noticed your ass from a whole in the ground, if I don't show it to you. I don't want any men talking to you and when I say I don't want any men, I mean I don't want any men. Your own brother could have been toting a message from a man."

"Are you serious?"

If looks could kill, I would have been dead. Seeing how this was going, I questioned, "You can't be that insecure about my love for you? I knew you were older the first time I ever saw you but that did not discourage me. If it doesn't bother me about you, then you shouldn't let it bother you."

"This isn't overboard. You haven't seen overboard," Marcus said.

He drove another half a mile before he started back speaking to me, "It seems like you don't think you are worth all this to me. I get the impression that you don't think you matter to me."

I decided to make him believe me by   saying, "I matter to you and I know I do."

"Then you don't know too much, Love. You are worth more if I could do more."

Chapter 12

I didn't say a word. Another half a mile went by, and I decided that it was either now or never. I stated in a calm tone, "Since you been off from work, your character has changed. You may need to go back to work."

"No. If you are implying that money is the problem; you are wrong. I have enough money for you and all my grandchildren to retire on for the rest of their generation."

"It's not about the money," I added to change his tone because the car was picking up momentum.

"Then what's it about?"

I looked straight ahead and saw how fast he was going. Fear set in as I said, "Marcus slow the car down. You are going too fast."

He began to act like he was going to hit every car coming our way head on. I was trying to hit breaks with no breaks on the passenger side. When that did not work, I scooted down to the floorboard as to hide. Mocking me he stated in a weak tone, "Slow the car down. Love, slow the car down. You are going too fast."

Marcus saw that he was really making frightful as he spoke in his own tone, "You aren't afraid of dying, are you? I mean you do pray and talk to God all the time; surely you are not afraid of a thing called death."

Peeping up at him, I beg, "That is not the case. Just slow the car down."

"What if I don't want to slow down?"

"I'm asking you to."

My husband looked at me, swirled to the side of the road, and snatched the car in park and yelled, "Get your scary self out and drive!"

He got out first and opened my door. He helped me out and closed his door. I got in and began driving. He didn't strap down. Marcus said as he looks straightforward, "I figured if I didn't let you drive, I'll kill us both."

My voice would not let me reply thank you. The rest of the ride home was quiet. I didn't like that but kept my nerves anyway. He stared out the window as I asked before making it home, "Why won't we go back to church?"

"You have been praying to God. HE must not be working for you because you want to go to the church you don't like?"

"I was just thinking that we haven't been in a while. You know we are not to forsake the assembly of believers."

"We haven't been since the girls moved away with their mother," he said in a down way.

"Yes, but that doesn't mean we can't go," I said in hopes he would say yes.

Marcus gave me that look that meant, later. The next few weeks flew by, and it was the eve of our anniversary. We were alone as usual in the living room when he asked a strange question, "You think that helper was cute don't you?"

He threw me off. I didn't know what he was talking about. I asked, "What helper?"

"The one at the Big and Tall Store; that helper."

"That was right at Thanksgiving, and I wasn't looking at him. My only person I was looking at was you, why?"

Out of nowhere, he asked, "You hungry?"

Whenever he changes the conversation that means I am to change the conversation and not bring it back up. Seeing what he has done, I complied to say, "No. You hungry?"

"I was sitting over here thinking about some barbecue. I haven't had it in a while and all of a sudden, I have the taste for some and plus it smells good this time of year?"

I really didn't want any, but I said, "I haven't had it in a while too. I guess I can go for some, as long as you cooking?"

"Yeah, I'm cooking."

"What you going to barbeque?"

"I want the finest steak, money can buy. I guess Rib eye and not T. Bone. Probably throw in your favorite, chicken on a stick and make a salad."

"You want me to help bring the steaks out the fridge or make the salad?"

"No, you can go on in the house and change clothes. I'll get the steaks for us."

He did not reply as I went in the house to change. I came back to the kitchen and was looking for the ingredients to make the salad. I could smell the barbeque smoke through the back door of the kitchen. I closed the cabinet then saw I didn't have the Ranch dressing. I opened the cabinet, took down the Ranch and was in the process of closing it, when I saw Marcus wearing his apron and a jug in his hand. He was not smiling as I placed the dressing on the table. Still, he did not say a word.

Not knowing what it was, but something made me stop and take heed to Marcus. I stared at him. He still did not say a word. He walked closer to me. I then realized in his hand was the jug of gas. Before I could run, I turned my head just in time when he drenched me with the gas fluid. I placed my hands up as to stop him. Like never before, I begged with tears and a sorrowful heart "Please don't do this to me. I don't want to die. Please, Marcus, please. I don't want to die."

With the look of anger and the feel of evil all around me, he spoke fiercely "You begging me or you begging a God that doesn't want to hear you?"

As God is my witness, I began to entreat him like never before, when I stated, "I'm begging you my love, in front of God not to do this. Please my Love, please don't do this to me. I'm sorry. I didn't mean to make you angry. I swear I didn't mean to do whatever it is I did. I'm so sorry, so sorry."

Throwing his weight, he spoke, "Why come? You don't think you are worthless to me?"

Still begging him, I trembled to say, "I am worth a lot to you. I know that now. Please, please don't do this."

Looking at his hand then back to me he said, "You say that now because I have these ingredients in my hand. What if I didn't have them? Would you still feel the same way?"

Shaking my head no with terror, I announced "That isn't so. I'm worth the world to you; with or without those ingredients."

He glanced around the kitchen and said, "What you think, I won't do it because we in this nice house? Screw this house! It can burn just like you."

"You are not thinking clearly. You are an educated man and very brilliant. You have a lot to live for. If not for me, think about your grandchildren" I tried to remind him.

Smiling in a cocky way, I heard him speak with so much pride, "Grandchildren I don't see. Surely you could come up with a better excuse than that? On the other hand, I am very intelligent, but love has no knowledge only feelings. You already saw how you look dead. Let me see how you would look burned."

I quickly decided to remind him again of the love he says he has for me by saying hysterically, "Marcus, you say you love me, so don't do this to me. You don't hurt those you love."

"Why not hurt those that you love? If I don't hurt you, you may think I don't love you."

"I've never thought that" I screamed back as tears were wetting me up.

Marcus took out the barbecue flame starter and flicked it. I began thinking about where to run or how to get by him. I know if I do the stop, drop and roll, he could throw more gas on me and burn me up completely. Fear set in as he stated, "You think the young punk would like you medium well or well done?"

"Neither Love neither. I don't want him. God knows I don't want him. I want you."

He walked towards me and replied, "You aren't just saying those things to me, are you?"

Like an Academy Award Winning Actress, I played the role of a lifetime, "Love I mean it. I have no one but you. I don't have my brother, I don't have the baby I lost, and I just have you. No man makes me feel like you do, and no man loves me like you do. Please, please think of the love you have for me; if you think of nothing else."

Marcus stopped walking. I guess he thought about it when he said, "I am your only family, aren't I?"

In the same manner of my begging, I agreed with everything that was in me, "Yes, yes, yes, yes, yes you are. You are my only family. My brother can't help me; he doesn't even talk to me. God doesn't hear me, but you know me and you hear me. You are my entirety."

He released the button, and the flame ceased. I never thought I would be any happier as I heard him declare, "Since you put it that way, wash that gas scent off you and come to the patio."

I scurried away quickly because I did not want him to change his mind. With the bedroom door opened, I heard him go out the kitchen door for the screen slammed. I wanted to close the bedroom door, but he has told me that he doesn't like closed doors unless he closes them. Undressing and going into the shower, I became painfully afraid of what he could do next. Doing my best to make up my mind, I decided to play his game. If I don't go along to get along, I will go mad and may end up dead or in jail.

The shower was short. I got out and went through my clothes. I was compelled to wear some joggers, a hooded sweatshirt with pockets and tennis shoes. I got dressed and sat there on the bed. I can't understand why I can't leave him. Today he soaked me to the skin in gas and could have burned me alive. Who would know I was dead? Who would miss me? The answer is no one. I am alone with him as my only family and the only one I talk too. I cried. I desire so much to leave him because I don't deserve to be treated like this. In fact, dogs are treated better. I can't do anything if it does not involve him, and I don't even have my own name.

I frowned as I thought, "Oh what is my name? Oh, it's Sarah." That is sad. I have not heard my name in a while, that I almost forgot my own name. He has called me Love or Child and sometimes Sarah but not enough to make me remember. I prayed, "Lord I've been calling on you for months and nothing has changed. One minute he is good, next he is great. In a blink of an eye, he is horrible and terrible. If you aren't going to remove me from this atmosphere, please God please change his ways. Forgive me if I am in error but I need you Almighty God. I am beginning to think that in order to hear from you; I must be bad. If that is the case, I am doomed. Please deliver me from the body of death. I don't think I can take it anymore."

I dried my eyes and hoped I wasn't gone too long. Sometimes I don't know what is too long. Too long could be whatever he says it is. He can get quick-tempered and hot headed like a snap of a finger. Funny as it is, I could be standing right there and wonder who else been here causing me problems. I don't know if I look at him wrong and he goes crazy or maybe I should take my chances and run. Either way, I feel damned if I go and damned if I stay. What is it going to take for me to wake up and realize that he doesn't love me?

Why can't I leave this ogre, I married? Why can't I see that he is only good as good is and according to the King James Bible, there is no good things in the flesh? However, it is leaving him I dread doing or just too afraid to do. Out loud I stated, "Jesus, I need you" and yet I heard nothing. With my husband I don't know how he can turn or when he can turn evil; all I know is that he will turn and turn quickly. Reality hit me, I'm still in here and he is waiting on me. Going back through the kitchen, I saw the scene and shuddered. Oddly enough, I can smell the barbecue smell.

Swallowing hard, taking a deep breath, clearing my mind and trying to put on a smile, I walked outside and saw he was barbecuing. I was still fearful as I kept my eye on him. My husband saw me watching him skillfully and smiled. He had the area decorated really nice. I hardly recognized our back patio; it was spectacular. He whispered, "Love, I did this while you were getting dressed. I wanted to surprise you because our anniversary tomorrow. I hope you like it."

"I do. It is lovely" I spoke with ease.

"Have a seat love."

I walked pass the grill and he laughed, "Don't get to close. I still smell a little gas on you."

I kind of laughed it off because if I acted any other way, he would be able to tell it and I don't want to bring any heat on me. Today I must start thinking what is best for me although, right now I don't know what the best is. But if I want to live, I must learn to calculate my every step. The Word say, "Watch as well as pray." I've been praying, now I need to learn how to watch.

I sat down and waited for him. Instead of fixing my plate right away, he said, "Love I want you to be able to survive on your own if the need be."

"What are you talking about?"

"I just don't want you to be alone and not know how to do anything."

"Where is this coming from?"

"It may sound crazy, but I was watching that family that got stranded on an island."

"Robinson Family," I added.

"Yeah, that's it."

"What about it?" I asked.

"They were stranded and they ran out of food and had to live off the fat of the land."

"Marcus, we don't ever take cruises like that."

"I know but it got me to thinking about you and how much of a city girl you are. There is so much you don't know, and you need to know. The survival rate of people lost in the woods is not good. They could fall in a snare, drown, get snake bitten and or freeze to death."

"I am so flattered that you are thinking of my safety."

"I always think of your safety, and I know you think of mine. Love that is why I love you so much and I also know these last few months have not been easy for you."

"No love they haven't," I said dryly as I thought about the coffin.

"I don't know what is going on with me when it comes to you. It's like I get angry just in my thoughts about you and I react to what is in my mind. Silly, isn't it?"

Thinking I've heard this before, I only replied, "No Love."

I got up and hugged him. Without releasing me, he held onto my hands as he spoke, "I care so much about you that it scares me at the extreme I would go to just to keep you to myself. I know you think evil of me because of the things I have done but please charge it to my head and not my heart."

"I know you love me and that is so important to me. I don't know where I would be without you. Marcus, you are all I have right now and all I need."

"You'll be dead if you don't have me, Love. That is where you will be. There is no way I could live knowing you are making another man smile in all the ways you make me smile. I cannot imagine not having you in my life."

"You say that all the time," I spoke to remind him.

"Well, I mean it; I can't have my entirety gone from me."

"No Love you can't because you're everything is right here for you as long as you will have her."

"I'm having her for all eternity," he said as he grinned.

"All eternity, it is."

He giggled as he responded, "Guess we stuck."

"Guess so."

"Love go sit down so I can bring you, your nutritious plate but I thought I would bring you an appetizer first."

"I hope its chocolate ice cream."

Chapter 13

Feeling more confident, I sat at the table as he fixed my plate. Moments later, he placed a beautiful bowl in front of me and said, "This is for you, Love."

I looked at it and was stunned. There was no steak on it. I had a bowl that actually smelled like dung with berries around it to make it look good. No matter how you dress up dung; it is still dung. The shape appeared to be like crap you see in a field, but we don't have a cow or a horse. I looked up and his plate had steak, baked potatoes, a chicken leg and a huge salad on the side, with tea. My stomach growled as I swallowed hard.

Taking my hand, I eased some berries in my hooded pocket, each time he bowed his head to eat. I wanted to make it look like I was eating the food. He looked up at me and gave me a smile to ask modestly "What? You don't like your plate?"

Not wanting to sound afraid, I spoke with a half-smile, "I love it, thank you."

"Good. I recalled how you told me that your mom told you to eat what's placed before you."

I didn't reply. He sounded extremely overjoyed as he pointed to my food, "That bowl you have had more nutrients and protein than that in my plate."

"Then why won't we share it together?" I replied in hopes I didn't say the wrong thing.

"What kind of man would I be if I took some of the best for myself and not let my better half having it all?"

"Love I want the best for you too. Let us share this nutritious bowl as a couple" I said as I looked at him in the face.

"That's okay. You go on and stop debating about your food and eat."

He sat there to see if I would eat. Going very extremely slow, I picked up a spoon and placed it on top of the dung. When I broke the patty in half, the smell made me gag. I am still at a wonder, why this man has placed dung on a platter for me? I know if I don't do as he requested, I will hate that I disobeyed him. Marcus encouraged me by saying, "Go on bite your steak patty because there is more in the outside freezer."

I picked up the spoon full and was about to bite with my eyes open. He said with joy, "If you eat it, I will beat it out you."

I froze and he laughed when his words came out his mouth, "I see you love me. You were about to eat a bowl of horse manure, just for me. Come here love."

He got up and laughed as he came towards me. I didn't know what to think as he wrapped his arms around me and pecked me on the cheek. I wanted to cry, scream and hit him but knew better. He said, "And you think I will let you go? You can't find a woman today that will do what they need to, but I have one."

Marcus then fixed me a real plate. I was so glad. We talked and talked as we ate the food. For hours I was having a great time with him. He took a break and talked to his daughters because they called him. He was very cordial and pleasant. It was nice to see him this happy and that made me happy. When he got off the phone, he and I made love out on the patio. It wasn't as passionate but great all the same. I am to the point, that my emotions are dead and numb from him. I don't even know what to think and if my brain didn't tell my lungs to breathe, I wouldn't breathe.

If I pretend that nothing happened than nothing happened. If I pretend what he does to me is ok, then I will be fine. If I wake up out of this way of thinking, there would be no way I would be able to be with him. Along the way, I fell asleep, and he woke me up with the words, "Happy Anniversary Love."

I turned over and he kissed me. The last three months has been hell for me. It's amazing how quick time passes when you have been fighting to live in a relationship that only you want. I yarned as he said, "Love it's three am. I want you to get up and put your clothes on, bring me a knife and meet me back here. We are going to do a creative art."

"What you have in mind Marcus?" I said trying to fight the sleep that was trying to get me.

"I want to you to learn the value of things."

"The value of what things?"

"Things that will make you spend the day without me?"

"Spend the day without you?"

"You will be spending it thinking of me."

"Love, I don't understand what you are saying."

"It's not for you to understand right now but you will or at least I hope you will."

"But."

"Shush, Love. Go do what I told you and hurry up."

I got up and put my clothes on. "Lord, I wonder what he has planned now." I went in the kitchen and got a knife. When I came back outside, he was standing up. I picked up the half bottle of water. He gave me a hug and said, "You cannot leave our twenty acres."

"What are you talking about? What twenty acres?"

"You are not to leave the property. You have to make it on your own and you better be back before the time in my head."

"What time in your head? I don't understand what you want me to do."

"Don't be back on time, that's what you do."

"Huh, wait. I don't understand."

He did not say another word. This time, from behind his back he brought forth the silver instrument, his gun. I thought I was seeing things at first until he said, "Run."

"What?"

Marcus pointed the gun in my direction and fired it. I ducked and screamed, "Are you crazy!"

"Yes, my darling. I am crazy about you. Now run!"

I took off like never before towards the woods. From all behind me I could hear him shooting. I don't even know where I am going, and I cannot believe he is shooting at me. Fact of the matter is nameless bullets are coming at me, says more than I think. I was running for my life as sticker briars tore at my clothing and hands. Never in my day, have I been on our property like this. Marcus comes out here often to hunt and fish while I have to stay inside. It mattered not, I was running and running. From a distance I could hear him behind me shouting, "Run Child, run."

The more he yelled at me, he would shoot. I couldn't tell if it's in the air or at me. I just ran and ran. I took few breaths because I don't know where he is at. I don't even know where I am at. All I know is, it's after three in the morning and I am in the woods trying to hide, from my husband. Now I get why he told me to take a knife, I assume to protect me or for food. Tears wanted to show up, but I stopped her! I can't afford to cry for someone that doesn't cry for me. I started back running, with that half a bottle of water in one hand and the knife in the other. I got tired and began to walk. My breath was coming back around as I did not hear him at all.

My stomach growled. I placed the knife under my arm and stuck my hand in my hooded pocket; to find the berries I hid at supper. Who would have thought these berries would taste this good? I ate and I ate. Taking a sip of water, I noticed that I liked my surroundings. The sun wasn't beaming down as hard, and the wind blew lightly. I could see squirrels running from tree to tree, just like I am. But the funny part is, if I wasn't trying to get away, I would love this type of day. I sat under a tree, on top of some pine leaves, I broke. Thank God I remembered how sitting on the plain ground would make you colder and drain all the heat from your body.

I don't recall how long I was under the tree. I don't recall falling asleep, but I knew it had to be past noon because how high the sun was in the sky. For me to be in a hurry to run, I actually felt at peace and at ease. Not only was I enjoying the day but I was happy. I didn't miss Marcus, and I didn't care if I ever saw him again. I've done from being head over heels in love, to not caring in love about my husband. Its' sad but true, my husband has changed me. I can see these things but to do something about it is something else. How can I leave? Better yet how can I stay and let him hurt me; perhaps kill me? Suddenly I became startled as I heard, "You thinking about me, Love?"

My heart nearly jumped out my chest as I tried to get up. Marcus snatched me onto my feet. He pulled me about two feet from the tree when he said, "You been here all day. Who are you meeting out here in the woods on my property!"

"No one!" I hollered.

"You supposed to have been at home by now. I didn't tell you to go this deep on the property."

"You know I don't know where I am. You just told me to run, and I did," as panic reached me.

"You say you don't, but you are full of surprises."

"Marcus, I am not lying to you. I swear."

"Swear when I'm done making you pay for cheating on me."

He threw my left side against the tree, which caused me to drop the knife. He saw it and spoke with anger, "You were trying to kill me, bitch!"

I was still on the ground on my knees, trying to catch my breath when I spoke, "No, it."

He initiated his full throttle attack on me by field goal kicking me in my side, twice at first. I glimpsed him raising his hands to say, "And the crowd goes wild!" before he kicked me two more times.

I was coughing and hurting. His size ten and a half shoe was making me pay for not coming home at a time, I knew not about. Laughingly he teased me, "I bet you won't pick up another knife and try to cut me with it."

He stopped kicking me and turned me around to say, "Now I get to kick the other side. I can't do one side and not the other; that side will get jealous?"

In the like same manner, he kicked me and kicked me. Marcus in short deep breaths stated, "You will learn to be submissive if it kills you. No other man will have you but me. No man!"

At this point, I am hurt and angry. I have devoted my life to this man, and he does this to me. I have prayed to the Lord and no answer but yet I am the good girl. This time he kicked me harder than ever. I believed I fell against the tree and hit my head. He laughed and mocked me, "You weak. You have all that education, all that praying and you are still weak! You are pathetic, that's what you are. No man wants you. No man will have you that is why I am with you."

Marcus kneeled down to devilishly whisper in my ear, "I can't stand the fact, that I love you. God, I wish I could kill you dead, but no one would come to your funeral because no one knows you exist. You are blank slate as the day you are born. You are nothing and you will never be anything without me."

If he was making this personal, he just did. A light came on in my head. I replayed his words back in my mind how he says how he can't stand the fact that he loves me? He can't stand the fact that he loves me! When I thought that, he lifted my head up and spat in my face. Upon releasing my head, I found my voice. Swallowing

227

as to wet my throat, I spoke as loud as my tone would let me, "LORD BE MY STRENGTH!"

My husband laughed at me and began mashing my hands as he stood on them. He teased what I spoke as he said, "HE been your strength the whole time and you still can't fight. You been talking to HIM and HE still hasn't given you anything but unanswered prayers."

Marcus taunted me by saying, "Come on get up! Get up! I bet you can't get up and have this super strength HE is supposed to give you. God doesn't hear a woman like you. HE turns his nose up when you call on HIS name."

I think he got an idea for he spoke with amusement, "Lord since you won't give her strength; give me strength to literally put my foot in her ass. Can you do that Jesus? Can you hear me, your child? The one on the ground doesn't have what it takes to get a prayer through, but I do. Hear me this day. Give me the ULTIMATE STRENGTH to put this here, right foot in her moon sharp ass. Amen, Jesus."

Marcus held my head up and said, "You better not fall before I get a good kick."

He went behind me to scoot my butt in the air. From what I could tell; he walked a good piece from me. Like a wind rushing to cool you off, I heard him running behind me full speed. The moment he lifted his leg to kick me, I moved, and he fell on his back with a hard smack. Marcus was moaning and groaning. I stagger to my feet with everything I had. Seeing he was halfway on his feet the fight or flight instinct kicked in and I wasn't running away.

Similar to a bull charging, I lowered my head, and I went for him. Contact was instantly when my head touched his stomach. Having so many feelings of love and hate; my anger put him back on the ground. Marcus was moaning more and more. I assumed he was dazed. I can't believe I am attacking him. More or less, I bet he can't believe I am attacking him. Like never before, I put my love for him to the side. I didn't think nor care how he would felt. I have built my life around him, segregated myself from my family just for him and the way he makes me feel. Nothing ever mattered so much in my life but making this man happy.

The more I thought about how he took my love for granted and how he made me insecure, shallow, defenseless, lonely, and dependent upon him for my life; made me revengeful. For once I am going to do me. I got up and for a moment, I stared into the face of the man I would have died for. Thinking about how he showed me love, I did as he did; I kicked and kicked him between the legs. I kicked the only tool he used to keep me emotionally hooked and under his spell, when he wasn't torturing me. It felt wonderful to fight back.

It was like a weightlifting off my shoulders. I had no idea that violence could be so wrong but feel so right. Now I have and idea how he feels when he does the things he does to me. At this moment, I am the hunter and not a prey. This overwhelming sensation or power gives you a rush like never before with feelings of not wanting to stop. Impartially I don't want to stop. Having this new irresistible urge to destroy my husband, I picked him up with strength; I knew not about. I then dropped him as hard as I could on a tree root, sticking out the ground. When his body came into contact with the earthly root, it made that disturbing sound.

He coughed as air escaped his lungs. With no regards, if he was ok, I picked up the knife and ran briskly away, while holding only one of my aching sides. No idea where I was headed, I just ran. All I know is I have to get far away from him, but it hurts me to breathe. I closed my eyes and did not look where I was going. Nevertheless, they opened when I fell in a stream, a small creek perhaps. The cold bitter water chilled me instantly. I emerged from the cold bath like a fish jumping out the water for a show. Shaking my head, I reached up and removed what water I could from my eyes.

I hollered as I came to my senses. I saw the bank and scarcely walked back to the dry land. Coughing and caring on, I could not relax. The nerves in my body were having a field day under my skin. My body is drenched with water, my eyes are somewhat muddy, and I am dirty. I am dazed, with no clear vision as to where I am at.

Inhaling deeply, I sat at the water banks to allow the sun to half dry me. I'm cold and I am alone. I have to get myself together. This time, my prayer was, "Lord if you let me live through this, I will be obedient to what I have to do for you; even if you never hear a prayer from me again."

I lain back on the bank and rested my eyes for a few. I cannot comprehend what is happening in my life; either he loves me, or he doesn't, either he is for me, or he is against me. I don't know what to think, if I can think. He has been confusing me since, he retired. He is too old for a mid-life crisis but not old enough for things to change. Thinking I heard a sound, I sprung up and saw it was nothing. I was still alone. A part of me wanted to run back and check on him but the other half dared me.

Pulling up my jacket, I check out my ribs. I could see the bruises as plain as day. I put it back down and the knife fell out. I picked it back up and put it back into my hooded pocket. The sun was starting to set. I am hungry and thirsty with only a knife because I left the half bottle of water back with Marcus. Standing to my feet with gruesome pain, I knew I had to keep it moving. My clothes were sort of dry as I walked and walked for what seemed like more hours. I am tired, hurt, hungry, bitter and thirsty. I spoke, "Lord help me, please help me. I have a knife, but I don't know how to kill with it."

By means of having the Lord to provide was a way out, it proved to be so. There before me, was a small bush of berries. I literally fell to my knees sobbing tears of joy. The Lord has provided food in my wilderness, like HIS Word says HE would. Rushing over to eat, I know longer thought about anything. I ate and ate until I was full. Now night encompassed me, and I am getting cold. I snug at the fact that my love and I were to be having our anniversary, but we aren't. Instead, we are in the woods playing a killer game of who gets caught. Feelings of love that I use to feel were gone.

In its' place is disgust, rage, hate and the deepest one; loathe. Here I am a woman that once had a thriving life is now filled with darkness, gloom and void. Memorizing, that once a math student of mine used a science project to relate to math. He was stating that if a person is high in a tree an item was dropped onto an object below, they won't be as hurt as bad; it depended on the velocity the object is dropped. I did the math. I am not bigger than Marcus, but he is barely taller with muscles.

Giving the right, velocity and height of a projected object, the smaller could crush the bigger. Looking around, my eyes followed the moon's beam. It showed me the most perfect tree. It stood out like a red thumb. My eyes never lost focus of that tree as I walked hurriedly. Once I arrived, I saw how, it stood about one hundred feet high with limbs as thin but grew thicker further up. "This is the one" I heard my mind say. To beat someone at their own game, you must think like them. Everything I hoped to accomplish is riding on him following me.

As I climbed the tree, I checked each limb for durability. I saw that it wouldn't take much to break the ones closer to the ground; therefore, I broke them as I climb further up. When I finished breaking the limbs, I stayed on the strongest branch and waited without sleeping. Dawn was at hand and my house was in view. I bet if I had binoculars, I could see clean to our patio. Looking down, I threw the knife onto the branches, I was happy because the knife landed perfectly. This bastard did this on purpose and now I am doing this on purpose. I knew he would tell me that he would be checking out the land and going fishing; I didn't know he raised fruit trees and had a creek.

I was almost exhausted from waiting because it is now daylight. I heard a hide and seek nursery rhyme, "Come out, and come out wherever you are. You can't run and you can't hide. Come out; come out wherever you are. You can't run and you can't hide."

It was Marcus. He had a thick stick in his hand that he swung fiercely to and from. I guess in case I was hiding in the nearby tall grass, he could hit me. I began to shake and had to calm myself because I don't need to mess this up. I did not make a sound. I stood still so he would not see me. I glanced down and had pure visual of him but needed him to move another foot or two over. I could have sworn he heard my heart beating as he sniffed the wind and said, "I can smell you

Child. Come out Love. The game is over. I miss you and I want us to celebrate our anniversary."

Chapter 14

I thought for a second and remembered our anniversary ended at midnight; so, he can keep that one. Finally, he moved the extra space I needed. He squatted for the knife, and I seized the moment, by jumping out the tree. He never saw me falling because he had his face towards the ground. When my knee hit him in the center of his back, he rolled onto his face. The student that gave me that idea truly deserved that A. I caught my breath, stood up and stood over him in the sun. He peeped through his eyes and said with pain, "You don't have the guts because you love me."

Leaning close just to make sure he hears me I replied, "No Love I didn't have the guts but loving you gave them to me."

I picked up his right leg and placed it against the tree. He grumbled, "What you doing?"

Still without words, I looked at him. I guess he realized what was about to happen as he said, "You wouldn't."

With a warm smile, I fell on it at the knee with all my might. He screamed a sound like no other as his leg dangled at the knee. The way that joint crackled as it ripped, is a noise I would not forget. Just seeing the blood through his pants would make you sick but then again, I'm sick because he made me this way. Yelling at the top of his lungs, "You crazy! You hear me! You crazy bitch!"

Seeing he is still being him, I shouted "No you invented me, remember. When I was sweet you made me sour, but this is crazy!"

I picked up his other leg and placed it also against the tree and I said, "You always doing things to me and I love you but now, I want to see you walk away from this."

As if I was made of cement, I jumped harder onto his knee. He cried in such agony as his leg twisted. When I got up to see my Love, he had passed out. Using the opportunity, I began to hit him repeatedly over and over to break his arms with the stick he had planned for me. I desired to cause severe injury to his hands and head. I didn't want to kill him, but I preferred to inflict harsh pain to him as he has done me. The main objective was whenever, it rained I wanted him to be reminded of me and what he put me through. Seeing, I haven't done enough, I used the stick again to strike his chin many times. I was trying to break his jaw and when I heard the crack; I knew I had succeeded.

I threw the stick down and began searching for the cell I know he has on him. I found the phone and just sat there for almost ten minutes before calling 911. Once I did, it hit me that I have done severe damage to my husband. I never wanted to hurt him so bad, but I did. I got beside him and cried as if I didn't do anything. About twenty minutes later the police and EMT found us. The police helped the emergency worker strap Marcus onto a gurney. They took him to the open field and air lifted us out.

A show for my life is now at hand. They would not believe how horrible this man I love has been to me; therefore, I must make this story a great one. When we got to the hospital, they rushed him into surgery. I was alone with my thoughts before the police came. When he did walk over to me, I asked impatiently, "Is he ok? Please tell me that he is ok."

"Ma'am I hope so but right now I have to ask you a few questions."

Shaking my head yes, I let the tears fall and I sat down in the seat. He sat beside me and stated, "Ma'am, I know you don't want to talk about this, but I have to while it is fresh on your mind."

Crying tears of lies, I replied, "Okay."

"What happened to your husband in the woods?"

I closed my eyes. I know by closing your eyes, it would appear that you are really trying to remember whatever happened. Taking a deep breath, I stated "It was our anniversary, and we wanted to do things different. He wanted to show me a beautiful view of our home from the inside of our property. I agreed to go. We took only a knife and a stick. We finally found the most beautiful spot to make love. I was going to climb up alone, but he wanted to show me personally how romantic it would be for us. I didn't want him to do it because I knew he was afraid of heights, but he told me it was something he wanted; I let him have his way. My love started climbing and climbing. He told me as he climbed that the limbs were somewhat weak, and he was glad that I did not come up. Soon as he stopped climbing, he looked down, and seen how far he was, from the ground. I assume he was well over fifty feet in the air, just by the distance. I yelled, now you can come down. He laughed as he turned around, the tree limb he was standing on snapped."

I let the tears roll. The officer spoke, "Take your time, Mrs. Grady."

Using tears of the events he had done to me, I continued, "I couldn't move and while he was falling, I began screaming. When he made it down, I ran to his side. I was unsure about what to do because he wasn't moving. I listened for his breathing and saw how faint it was. I began searching for our phone. I got so afraid, Officer but somehow, I got service and called for help. The lady said help was on the way. I ran back to him, and I checked again to see if he was alert, and he wasn't."

Tears came like a hurricane as I cried. The Officer placed his hand on me to say, "Ma'am I hope he heals fast and trust the doctor is doing all he can."

"Thank you, officer, I have to go check on my husband," I said between sniffles.

It took him twenty minutes to talk to me because I kept crying between the lies, I was telling. The officer finally left, and the nurses acted like they could not tell me anything after being here for almost five hours. Soon as I stood up to inquire of Marcus, I saw a doctor. He said, "Mrs. Grady?"

I turned and ran to him like I was winning a race. He said, "He has two severely broken legs, a broken jaw, a severe concussion and a few crack ribs. We stopped the bleeding in the brain, and we have him in ICU. This is a precaution because blood clots could form, and he could die."

"He's going to die!" in real fear.

"No, at this present time; however, his mouth will be wired shut and it will take extensive physical surgery."

"Will he be able to walk, talk; move his arms? Tell me something!"

"As for the walking, he will have screws maybe not permanent. We have his legs in swings to keep them elevated. I do believe he will be in the hospital for a while, unless you have insurance to move him home and have physical therapy come there. I don't know your financial state, but all these are options. Someone from the hospital can give you more details on what you need to do. Now as for your husband talking, that also is undetermined and depends on how much he wants it. Coming from the medical standpoint, I say he may not be able to walk, talk or move his arms perfect. I have to be absolutely honest with you. His arms are battered, just like his legs. I guess he is up in age; therefore, his bones broke easily. Again, he may not move his arms as much for months. How well he is able to do that is beyond me but from a medical point of view, it's going to take a lot of time and a lot of prayers."

"Is he conscious?"

"No, we have to keep him knocked out because awake he would be in so much pain. He opened his eyes but went back out. I want you to know that he may not remember because he took a nasty beating to the head."

"He may not remember. Oh, God don't tell me that!"

"Mrs. Grady, he may not remember anything before this because he did take a beating from those tree limbs. Again ma'am, he remembering things is like his ability to get well; it all depends on him."

Sounding terrified, I spoke with many emotions, "When can I see him, doctor? I need to see my husband!"

"You can see him now. Go through those doors. A nurse will show you how to wash up and put on the protected clothing."

I took out and went as he directed. I became steps away from his room and was not sure if I wanted to go in. I was not scared; I just didn't have any emotions. Easing the door open, I saw he was out of it. It was an awful sight. Taking my time, I walked up to his bed and sat beside him. I touched him and spoke softly, "There is so much more waiting on you when I get you home."

He twitched and jumped like he was frightened. Honestly, I admired that sight. For the next few days, Marcus was in and out of conscious and I was right by his side. If they all wanted to see a devoted wife, they were looking at her. I wasn't going to leave him for nothing. Every day I read to him and showered him with so much affection that I didn't know still existed. Sometimes Marcus would smile at me, and I would be so happy.

Following the long stay at the hospital from December to March, Marcus was finally allowed to come home. I had arranged for physical therapy to come out every day along with a nurse to bathe him five days a week. I cleared out the living room and put him in it with me on the day

245

bed. I had him where he had that coffin at as a reminder to me how he did me. I shook at that thought for I am still traumatized from that. Soon as we were settled, I asked, "You hungry, love?"

He nodded, yes and spoke it a little. I replied, "Me too. What would you like?"

He began talking some through his teeth. I spoke, "I can't understand you. But I have a very nutritious meal for you."

I went in the kitchen and brought in the same bowl of food he prepared for me a while back. It was the bowl of dung with a few berries missing. He didn't say a word. He turned up his nose at it. I laughed just like he used to. I picked up a spoon full and said, "You once told me how good and healthy this is. Don't you want to get well?"

He whispered through the wiring, "Yes."

"Okay. This is a very nutritious meal that a wife gives her husband. Open your mouth the way they taught you."

He opened his mouth, and I was about to put it in his mouth but put it back in the bowl. I spoke, "Awe Love. You were about to eat that for me? You don't have to eat that. Here is some apple sauce for you and if you a good boy, I may bathe you."

I fed him the apple sauce. I know he is still hungry because his stomach growled. I fixed me some spaghetti, one of his favorite meals. Eying me like a hound, I teased, "I would offer you some, but you can't open your mouth and say please."

I saw him trying but he couldn't. I laughed in his face. I yelled out, "Now the tables are turned. How you feel now?"

He didn't say anything. I said, "Do you not recall how you used to beat on me and scare me to death? Or do you want me to help you like you didn't help me?"

He was quiet as if he was actually trying to remember. Shortly after finishing he kept staring. I said, "Here maybe I won't get in trouble for giving you this."

Swiping the bowl with my hand, I put it in his mouth, and he sucked on it like it was the best tasting thing to him. He was reaching for it, and I took it away and put it in the kitchen. I got him ready for bed and he only stared at me. I asked, "You need me to help you speak?"

He glared at me as I said, "Well whatever it is, it'll have to wait. I don't have time to play mind games."

I turned the lights off and went to sleep. The next day, the CNA came in and bathed him; I even helped. About an hour later, the physical therapist came. They showed him how to use a walker. I would even be caring as the evil parts of me began to die. I really didn't like being hurtful to my husband but all I could think about was how he was to me. It was like I couldn't let the past go and I really didn't want it to leave me. Even his children were calling him because they haven't heard from him.

I told his daughters that he had left me for another woman, and they stopped calling. As God intervened, I felt sorry and called Elisabeth and told her that he had an accident and how the other woman didn't want him, and I took him back. She told her sisters and over the next few weeks, his daughters began calling. A few more weeks past and Marcus's cell phone rung. It was Elisabeth. I picked up and she said, "Thank you for picking up, Sarah."

I listened as she said, "Please listen. You don't have to talk but please hear me out."

"I have a few minutes, talk."

"I can only speak on my behalf, but I don't have a problem with you, I never had. I know you think I do but I don't. It is true. I resent the fact that he married a younger woman, but I can't change if he loves you and you him. I don't know how things are now, but I want you to forgive me for any wrongdoing I may have done to you."

She caught me off guard as I spoke, "That means a lot for me to hear you say that. Elisabeth, you are forgiven."

"Thank you so much Sarah. I feel that I can breathe now."

"You're welcome."

The line was quiet as she asked, "How is my dad?"

"He is doing better. In fact, he is doing very well."

"Thank you, Sarah, for taking care of him, in spite of him marrying you then leaving you for another woman."

Silently I spoke, "Goodbye Elisabeth. I have to go back and tend to your father."

"Goodbye Sarah."

I didn't have to tell her the real story and frankly it's none of anyone's business. I hung up went outside and watched the workers work with Marcus. They left and the pathologist came, and she was making him talk more. His words were coming around but were slurred. Every so often, he would reach up and touch his sore jaw. The Lord is really working with him, and I don't get it. I thought how is it that Marcus is doing so well and when I needed deliverance I could not get delivered? It seems like he is getting all the help that I asked for but didn't get it. I stormed out the area and went in the house by the front window. I battled in my mind how he could be so blessed and yet, be so hateful? "Lord please remove this feeling away from me. I know you are a just God but help me to overcome these emotions. I don't know if what I feel is right or not because of what I have been through. Amen."

The warm sun was great on me. It made me feel happy as I recalled that day in the woods and how I sat under the tree delighting myself. That day was perfect even if I had to run. When that came to mind, I shut off my thoughts. Granting, that Marcus was still not able to walk, talk, move or remember perfectly, I was still embarrassed about the way he did me; how I did him. His maltreatment continues to haunt me, afresh. It disturbs me because I did this to him. I do think my actions were justified and righteously done. He was trying to kill me, and I had to defend myself by all means.

For a long time, I tried to rationalize my actions and each time, I didn't see myself doing any different, even if I wanted too. I could still hear him shooting at me. I could remember all the things he did to torture me, but I didn't leave. I just buried it in my mind about the life he and I had after his retirement and focus more on what is happening now. Marcus was improving; although, I didn't like it. He would go to sleep reading the bible and wake up reading the bible. A new him was emerging and I didn't like it. I did not like how I was becoming like him daily; even when I tried not to. To me a similar Marcus had been born in the woods on that December day.

When I mistreated him, I would feel bad then I would remember how he didn't feel bad for mistreating me. I didn't like the way I treated him or doing all that lying to myself. I was getting tired of making up excuses for the way I was bringing him pain. As I put Marcus to bed, my thoughts brought the Lord Jesus to mind and how people mistreated HIM and yet; HE forgave them. I know I must possess that same love, but it is hard. It seemed like it was easier and better to be hateful to him. I wasn't me; I was him.

I went to bed with a heavy heart and a weary mind. I began crying myself to sleep. During this sleep, I thought back to our Pastor. I clearly remembered one of his messages when he said,

"The easiest thing in the world to do is to give up and the hardest thing in the world to do is to forgive and forget those that has wronged you. It takes something to truly forgive someone. I don't mean you forgive then bring it back up; that is not true forgiveness. Whatever that person has done to you can stay on your mind, rob your feelings and plague your heart. It will invade you, consume you and eventually take over your everyday life. That is because you are still in the flesh and have not truly trusted God for what HE can do. Many times, the reason for not forgiving is because you want them to hurt like you did but vengeance is the Lords and not yours. Think of this term, if you can't forgive, how can you expect to be forgiven? It doesn't matter if you didn't do someone else like you were done, forgiveness is forgiveness. I'm not saying you will right out forget the wrong, because you won't; it'll take time and dedication for that to happen. Out front, I'm saying don't let the wrong get to you. Have your hands clean before God. Make sure you are in good standings with HIM. Do your part. Ask the Lord Jesus to remove any and all barriers that is hindering your spiritual growth, your life. Ask HIM to heal your heart and cleanse your mind of the wrong.

HE can't do anything until you let it all go. You have to give it to Jesus and ask whoever wronged you to forgive you. It may not seem like the right thing to do, but it is the best thing you can do. Get free, let it go and let God have control."

At this point, my eyes flew open, and tears fell. I know now I have to ask Marcus to forgive me so I can be free to love my husband as I need too. It didn't seem right, but it is what I must do. This time when I awoke, I had a new outlook. I went to area where Marcus was. I was nervous and afraid but confident because I know this is what my Heavenly Father would want me to do. Soon as he saw me, I spoke assuredly, "I must confess to you. You treated me like an outsider from October to December. I know you may not remember how things were between us, but they were horrible. You didn't use to be that way but when you quit working you became difficult to live with. I would be afraid to go to sleep because I would hear you make a gun click. You've shot at me; you've put me in a coffin, and you have done so much damage to me; yet I could not leave you. I actually thought things were wrong with me for staying with you after all you have done. No answer ever came to my mind about why I am still here. You separated me from my brother, your children don't like me, I had to quit my job, and no one was allowed to call me but you. You've let a woman suck on your crotch; yet I am still here. To be honest, I had nowhere to go and there wasn't anywhere I wanted to go. Marcus, you became everything, my world, my life. I could not imagine myself without you because I have been with you. That day you got hurt in the woods, I wanted you gone because of how you treated me. But I love you. Out of all the things you did to me, I loved you."

He gave me that look that he normally gives me when he is thinking of doing bizarre things to me. I got up and ran to the patio to cool off. He is vulnerable and I am still fearful of him. He makes me want to do to him what he did to me, but it won't be right. I look at him and can't stand him but yet I love him so much. In my mind, I can do some damage to him while he is like he is but that too won't be right. This man whom my feelings, my beings adore is the same man I hate as much as I love him. How can the two feelings interlock? How can I feel one way about him then the opposite the next?

Being deep in thought, my eyes focused on that tall tree. It's weird how I never seen that tree before until now. I sat there for almost an hour, thinking about my marriage and wondering where I go from here. Then I heard a bump coming from inside. I rose up and saw Marcus. He was doing his best to come outside with his walker. I was half happy. I was glad he was improving; just hoped the old him didn't return. I got up and opened the door. I smiled as I said, "Love you are doing so well.

I helped him outside, to sit alongside me. We didn't say a word as we sat there staring out onto our property. I don't know what he was thinking but I was thinking about the last time we both were out here and that was the day that changed my life and my thought process. I asked, "You want tea or your favorite, hot chocolate with marshmallows?"

"Hot chocolate."

Leaving him outside, I went inside and fixed us a cup of hot chocolate. I came back and he was practicing how to talk as the lady was teaching him. Marcus is getting the very best help that money can buy, and it is paying off. He must have the determination; I thought as the doctor's words came back to my mind. To see him responding so well is amazing. We sat there drinking as he listened to me talk and talk. He would even smile as I talked. Marcus even made word sounds that I could understand; when he did so correctly, I would give him a hug or even a light kiss on the cheek. This atmosphere is the most peaceful I have had in months, and I was really enjoying it. My husband would reach for my hands time after time.

Time after time I would help him move them. When I let go of his arm, he with his shaking hand reached for mine. I squeezed it and he bowed his head; for an indication to pray. I said, "Lord, we ask you to forgive us of our sins, known and unknown. We know we have been done unjust, and we have been unjust, but we ask

257

this day for newness. My husband and I can't do it without you. Jesus, you know our hearts and our intentions. You know we didn't mean to do what we did but we can't change it. You alone know our thoughts before we think it and you know what we are in need of before we ask. This day we ask for you to work the kinks out of this marriage with the letter R. Rebuild the love that was torn, Rework our communication lines, Rewind in our minds about the love we once shared and Rebuke the anger spirit that tried to attack us and give us Renowned strength to do what we must; in your name Jesus, Amen."

Chapter 15

Marcus was holding onto my hand harder. It all started when I asked the Lord to give us strength. He was accurately trembling like a leaf in the winds. I didn't know what came over him, but he started crying. I removed my hand to wipe away his tears. He looked up at me. In his face I justly saw authenticity and love. His eyes became filled with tears as I heard plain as day, "Forgive me for the pain, Sarah."

My ears never thought they would ever hear those words. Now my eyes are watery, and my heart is beating just as fast as I got in front of him and touched his face to say, "No Marcus, forgive me for the pain."

Over the next few months November came again. All his therapy was down to once a month because he walks on a cane and his speech isn't all that, but it is understandable. We haven't made love since that night, and I am kind of glad of that but he sleeping in the bed with me makes my body yearn for him. When the urge to have him comes over me, I look at me lying in the coffin and all those fuzzy feelings vanish. He hasn't had the idea to come at me, but I know it is coming.

This morning, we got ready for service. He doesn't like me helping him get ready. Marcus wants to do it on his own and for the most he does. There are times, when he gets frustrated, and I have to help him. He would pull me close to him and hold me. It is so right to be in his arms even if I tried to tear them off his body. He sensed something was bothering me and he asked, "What bother's you Sarah?"

I gave my husband a smile when I said, "This is like a dream that I am afraid I will have to wake up from."

"I must have been something serious to you?" he asked innocently.

"You became cruel when you retired. Before then you were so good to me."

"I have another chance to make it better for you," he spoke as if he meant it.

"You loving me is better for me, Marcus; even if I don't want to admit it."

He spoke, "I will."

We left for service, and I saw his children, Tonya and Elisabeth. I almost forgotten they moved back to town and the others were coming to visit. After every service, it still sickened me to see them all gathered around him like a celebrity. They would try to baby him as if I am not doing a good job in watching out for him. Keeping the comments to myself, I continued on being the happy wife. Service after service, it was getting to me. I would purposely talk to the pastor and his wife just so I could not witness him being so kind. I want the people to see him the way I saw him for the last three months before our anniversary. They only see a man that the Lord has been healing miraculously. They hear him testifying in service how good God has been to help him make it through the ordeal and thus far they are blind like I once was.

Why can't they see him, Lord? I used to question in service. Why can't someone who is supposed to be spirit filled pick up on his attributes before the incident? Every time, I would hear someone exclaimed how blessed or gracious the Lord has worked on his behalf, I would grit my teeth. The whole while, knowing he was once manipulative. I don't have a clue as to what is going on with me. I am used to the way he is now because that is how he was before our anniversary but prior to that date, he was a monster behind those doors. If those walls could talk, they would make everyone cringe at the horror I had endured with my husband. The harder I prayed the madder I would become.

I want him to stay the way he is, but I can't let go of the past. I can't stop thinking about the way he teased me and petrified me for those months. I have been praying but don't know why it is so hard for me to let how he did me go. I've read scriptures and nothing has worked. Then one day as he and I were sitting at the table, he stated in a littler clearer voice "I feel like I am losing you. Am I?"

"To tell you the truth, I don't want you to lose me either, but you are correct."

"I can't remember all how I was before all this but from your point of view I must have been ruthless."

Staring at him I spoke, "You were. I guess that is why I can't forget as easily."

"We both have asked for forgiveness and that is all we can do."

"I know we have but I am a woman, and it may take a little more time for me, than you. Marcus, you really stressed me."

"Sarah, we are going to be better than ever, wait and see. I will spend the rest of my life making it up to you, I promise I will."

"Marcus just be patient with me. I'll be back to the old me in no time."

"Where else am I going? You are my world, Sarah."

Hearing his stomach growl, I asked with a smile "You hungry?"

"How about Chinese?" he asked.

I paused for a second and replied, "Sure why not."

I was glad I went because I had a chance to bring home a different variety. I still don't like Chinese, and he must not remember. I left to go get the food. I want to surprise him and show him how much I care for him. Making sure, he was in the kitchen when I came back, I came in to say, "Close your eyes and do not open them. I have a surprise for you."

"Sarah, you don't have to do this," he said as if he was a child.

"I know but I thought this would be wonderful."

He closed his eyes, and I made numerous trips to the car to get all the pre-ordered food. Once I sat the table I screamed, "Open your eyes."

Marcus opened his eyes and smiled as he asked, "What is all this? You were to go get Chinese."

"I know but it is Thanksgiving, and we never had a real Thanksgiving."

"It's Thanksgiving?" he questioned with a puzzled expression.

I stated, "Last year we didn't have it because we went shopping and the girls were with their mother in Georgia."

"Shopping?" he questioned.

"Let me finish setting up. Then we can talk."

"Ok. Hurry up. I am anxious to know about the things we did."

I washed my hands. I put the plates in front of us and my husband blessed the food. I fixed my food, and he wanted to fix his, which, he did a great job doing so. He said, "You were gone for a while, and I got worried about you?"

"The lady at the deli was filling orders as I was there to pick up ours."

"As you were saying."

"Oh, yeah. We went to the big and tall store across town, and you got in an altercation."

"Someone fought me?" he asked in a surprising manner.

"You started it and beat the young man up."

"Why I beat him up? Why was I ever fighting?"

"Slow down and let me answer your questions in one sentence. You didn't want him talking to me."

"Seriously, I did that?"

"Yes! You didn't want any man talking to me."

"I do sound awful."

"Marcus, for the last few months, of last year, we didn't socialize with people."

"Not even my daughters?"

"No. They didn't like me" I said because it was of the truth.

"Why not? You are everything and then some to me."

"You always said that, Marcus."

"Has to be the truth, then?"

"Eat up; your food is getting cold."

We ate in silence for a few more minutes before I asked, "You like it?"

"Sarah I am surprised at you, and I love it. Thank you."

He and I ate a few moments more before he asked, "What we do for December?"

I nearly choked because that is our anniversary month. Slowly he asked, "You, ok?"

Gulping down the tea, I spoke with a crackled voice, "Yeah, the food went down the wrong way. What were you asking?"

Marcus said, "What we do for Christmas in December?"

"We normally celebrate our anniversary the whole month of December and we usually celebrate it doing nontraditional stuff."

"What we do last year?" he asked.

Choosing my words carefully, I replied "Last year the night before our anniversary, we had a barbecue and the next morning while we were in the woods, you had your accident."

Marcus was quiet as I stated that. I touched his hands and said, "That was last year. This is a new year, a new beginning and a new us. That is the only thing we are placing our minds on."

I gave him a warm glow, when I said, "You right as always."

We finished eating and Marcus took his time and walked to the living room. He stood there and stared into the open space. I wanted to ask what he was looking at but feared he could remember. I continued cleaning up as he stood there. Then he sat in his favorite chair and asked, "Did I like this chair because it feels just right?"

"Yes, you loved that chair," I said.

"Oh, ok."

"Why did you remember something?"

"No but I liked that chair."

I finished my cleaning and Marcus said, "I'm ready to go to bed."

"You need my help?" I asked.

"No, I just want to hold you."

"I will be right on."

In a deeper voice, he commanded, "Could you come on now, please."

My soul trembled because his tone sounded like the old him. I walked towards him and almost fell, "You, ok?" he asked.

"Yeah, I'm good. Let's go to bed as you stated."

It didn't feel right. Marcus went in the room first. I went behind him and went in the bathroom. When I came out, the room was dark, and I could not see him. Fear kicked in. I walked unhurriedly and he asked, "What is wrong with you?"

"I didn't know where you were, that's all," I replied in a fearful way.

"I'm lying in bed, waiting on you why?"

"Nothing at all, I just couldn't see you and I didn't know if you had gone back to the kitchen for some tap water."

"Nah, I'm still here," he spoke.

I got in the bed and faced him. He asked, "Can you turn around and let me hold you?"

I didn't want to do that because he used to sleep with me in a sleepers hold, and I was beginning to not feel at ease. Gently he placed his arms about my waist and asked, "You cold? You are trembling?"

"Yes, I am cold" I lied.

"It is a bit cold in here."

Marcus proceeded to get up and I asked frantically, "Where are you going?"

"I want to turn the heat up. I can't have my lovely wife cold."

"I can get it, if you want me to?"

"I'm up. I'll get it."

He went out the room with his cane and I prayed, "Lord please hear my cry. I feel so scared of my husband and I don't know why. Although he has shown signs of change, I still don't trust it as I should. Oh, Lord help me. Please God help me."

"Who were you talking too?"

"I was just praying" I said.

"Praying for what?"

Lightly I said, "Strength."

He stared at me in the bed before sitting on the edge. Then he got in. He spoke, "I was waiting to see if the room got heated for you before getting back in bed."

"Thank you Love."

"Anything for you," he spoke in his familiar tone.

My eyes bucked. I sat up and said, "You know what?"

"Yes, Sarah."

"I am not as sleepy as I thought I was. I am going to sit up in the chair over there and read," I spoke.

"You can lie in bed and read with your night lamp."

"I don't want the light to bother you from getting your rest."

271

"Sarah, I want you near. I insist you lying in bed to read the Word. In fact, you can read it to me so I can go to sleep."

I got up and got my King James Bible. Walking back to the bed, I saw my little club was still beside me in case I need it. Nervously, I got back in bed, but I sat up and turned my night lamp on. He cuddled next to me and placed his heavy arm across my stomach. I was almost terrified to breath. To my memory, I recalled how he doesn't know any of it; I let out a breath of air. Once I began reading, about Noah. Marcus began to snore. I essentially felt good. Now that I am tired, I turned off the light and turned towards him. When he turned, I turned. I didn't skip a beat. All night we slept in a bed that could have been mistaken for a dance act. When the sun peeped into my room, I was relieved.

The Christmas atmosphere began taking over the house. From time to time, Marcus would say or do something that brought back to my mind how the old Marcus did me this time of year. But he hasn't given me any indication that he is lying. Going to bed, I wrapped my arms around him and slept. The next morning, I noticed that Marcus was already out of bed. My heart began jumping because I didn't even know he got up. At one point, I thought I saw him walking out the room but was too tired to debate with my mind, so I went back to sleep. Seconds later he came in and said, "I cooked for us, get up and change so we can eat together."

Should I even eat? I thought as I got dressed slowly. I came out of the room, and he had the table set. I smiled as he said, "You surprised me all the time and you do a lot for me. I wanted to return the favor to show you that I do appreciate you for all your hard work and not only that, but you have stuck by me through it all. For that I am so thankful that I am married to you, and this is all I came up with."

Slowly I said, "You have hash browns, eggs, waffles, bacon, strawberries and orange juice. This is my favorite breakfast."

"I kind of remembered when I looked in the fridge and saw all this."

"I am so proud of you, Marcus."

"It means a lot to hear you say that."

Chapter 16

We sat down and dove off into the wonderful breakfast. His conversations were pleasant and intriguing. He was talking on an educational level, and it was great; even though, he would stumble on his words from time to time. We left the table and sat on the patio. I didn't want to do it because I could see that tall tree. It's like it haunts me to recall how evil I turned in the woods. Marcus on the other hand loved the patio more than anything. We got up and went in. We talked more and more of us and our future. I even told him about the one time I did conceive. I could see the pain in his face as I told him what all happened. Not wanting to spoil our mood, he put on Christmas songs, and we sat on the couch singing.

"Go in the room and put on some warmer clothes and meet me outside."

Sounding in a teasing tone, I replied "Ok."

It was almost five o'clock in the evening and my love went to the patio. I saw that he was trying to light the patio fire pit. Before I could help, he did it. Sighing, I continued to watch. He had a thick blanket for us to cuddle under and a tin picture of hot cocoa. Marcus sat down and saw me at the door smiling. Marcus patted for me to sit beside him. He had his throw on his legs as he smiled at me with love. I sat beside him, and he tried to lift his arms. I helped him lift his arm around me. I placed my head on his shoulder and felt so comfortable.

"I wanted to make love to you out here under the stars as a witness to our new beginning. I may not be able to move like I used to, but I want to try. I know it has been a year since we were intimate and I know you are a young woman. Hell, I am an old man but seeing your body does something to my heart as well as my body."

Truthfully, I said, "Love, I married you because I love you, not for your age. I can wait until you are ready."

"I know you can, but I can't wait to have you. I tremble with need of it but what can I do? My legs don't cooperate at times and my arms can't hold my weight as they once did."

"Allow me to make love to you, Marcus," I spoke with my mouth. I know if I don't do this now, I may not ever want him to touch me again. I have a lot of mixed sentiments going on and sleeping with him is the last thing, I need to do; not want to do.

Suddenly I saw the fire was glowing dim, I asked, "Want me to add another piece to the fire?"

"I can try," he said.

I spoke, "I'll do it you go to the bathroom."

I got up and went to the small box of sticks. Marcus got up and began walking slowly. I picked up a thin stick and used both of my hands to break it in half. I saw Marcus stopped in his steps. He started back walking as I took another one and broke it. This time, he nearly fell. I asked, "You, ok?"

I saw that he took a deep breath before saying weakly, "I made a bad step."

He went through the kitchen door, and I closed the fire pit lid. It made a loud sound, but I thought it was Marcus falling so I yelled, "You, ok?"

He yelled out faintly, "Yeah, my leg felt weak. Be out in a minute."

"Oh, ok. Hurry up. I'm getting cold without you out here with me."

While he was in the bathroom, I saw how the night started out, cold but the wind has picked up. It feels like it may rain or sleet. After being outside longer, I got up to check on Marcus. When I made it to the door, so did he. I went back to my seat and sat down. I waited until Marcus was under the cover with me before saying, "I was about to come looking for you."

"I'm slow but I can manage" he said as he pecked my head and held the scent of my hair longer. Before I could pull all the way from him, Marcus said in his usual voice, "I want to take you somewhere."

"Ok, when?"

"Now."

"It's late" I stated to him.

"I know it is late but when I am with you there is no time."

"You always say things like that."

"It's because I mean it."

"Where you want to go?" I questioned.

"It's a romantic spot that Elisabeth told me about, when she talked to me. She was supposed to check it out but so far, I don't think she has."

We headed towards the car, and he went to the driver side. I asked, "You sure you up to driving? If you tell me where to go, I can drive us."

"I believe I am. At least I want to try."

"Ok. If you can't handle it, let me know and I will take over for you."

"Okay," he said as we got in the car. He began to drive and drive. I had never seen this part of town before, but he said, "It's beautiful out here, isn't it?"

"It is," I added.

Marcus drove a few more miles into the beautiful countryside. It was indeed beautiful as he said it was. My first thought is, he wants to make love like we used too but he parked the car. I got out and so did he. The wind was blowing the cold air all around us. I felt cold as I tighten my jacket on me. My husband pulled me close, pecked my forehead and smelled the scent of my hair. He stated, "Are you crazy bitch?"

Then he was quiet. It hit me. He remembered what I did to him. I tried to run from him but he twisted my arm tighter, using the most super strength. We were like Siamese twins he stated to my face, "For months, things would come and go. It wasn't until you broke those sticks that I remembered. I had to go to the bathroom to clear my head and think. That day in the woods, a year ago; you broke me down like an animal. You literally broke me down and it took a lot of money and willpower for me to get where I am at now. I must admit, you were clever than I thought. I had no idea that you would break me up as you did but you did."

"Marcus you were hunting me first. I was already afraid of you, but you insisted by shooting at me."

He stated slowly with hatred, "I didn't break you down."

"You broke me down mentally not physically. You played games with my mind and my heart."

"Games?"

"Yes."

"I got one for you. It's called I did it myself."

My eyes bucked when I heard the last part. My heart was in my ears as he laughed in an evil manner. He yelled, "You heard me right. I brought you out here to kill you!"

The entire time, I was looking for something to hit him with. I found nothing. I asked, "What about all that praying for us to make things right and believing in God?"

"What about HIM?"

I was appalled as he spoke, "You still easy to read and easy to get too. You seemed to have forgotten who made the rules you played by."

"Marcus haven't we reconciled?"

"You reconciled. I haven't forgotten how you did me. You literally broke me up! Can you imagine how to walk again? How about learning how to talk or move my arms. You made me live in agony for almost a year and you don't think that once I remembered that I wasn't going to get that ass?"

"You must have a short memory. You did me worse," I tried to make him remember.

"You could have done me the same way, but you choose not too and that is your fault," he said with hatred in his tone.

"My fault is that I believed you love me."

"Oh, but I did and still do, to some degree. Even when you mistreated me, I still didn't want any other man to you. Even that physical therapist kept at you, but you were too gullible.
You having those men around you drove me to

get better. I defied all odds and it's the evil in me that helped me."

"No, The Lord Jesus did, in regards to how you treated me. HE healed you."

"I don't believe as you believe."

My mouth fell opened; he spoke "I've surprised you again, haven't I?"

"Yes, but why kill me? Haven't you psychologically damaged me enough? You had almost succeeded in making me like you, but Jesus came back into my life and stopped it."

"No. Sarah when you create something you destroy what you create. You are my personal creation, and I will destroy you."

A tear fell. He said with no remorse, "It's too late for crying. You should have done that the day you said I do. If you make any rash movement, I will not hesitate to shoot you in the back and paralyze you. So, walk very slow. Then again, me taking care of you sound as nice as you taking care of me."

"I didn't mistreat you all the time."

"I can see, and I saw how you would look at me with hatred. I felt it in my soul; what your words would never say."

"What do you think after all you have done to mess with my mind?" I said with tears.

"I could have stopped but I was having so much fun treating you the way I did. Whenever I was depressed about my children not being around or something, torturing you always made me feel better."

I stood there still in shocked as he walked to the back of the car and got a flashlight. He called for me to come to the back, but I took off and he fired at me. I thought I was hit. He walked over and towered over me. He threw the shovel to the ground as he pointed the gun at me.

"The next time you disobey, I will outright kill you. Now get up."

I did but I was quivering. He yelled, "Pick the shovel up and don't get any bright ideas. I came here to kill you so don't make me do it sooner than I planned."

I got the shovel, and he yelled, "Walk."

All the time we walked, he was telling me about all the things he did to me. If he wanted to scare me all over again, it was working. He was having as much pleasure reminiscing about all the things he had done to me. I am now realizing that as much as I didn't want to go on, I should have because now my physical fate is in his hands.

Present Time
Chapter 17

With that gun towards me and being off in that hole made me think a lot of things and asking the Lord for help was the main thing. I knew that I myself could not do it because if that was the case, I would have left him that night he poured soap on me. I stayed. However, watching him on his knees looking down at me made me fearful especially when Marcus pointed the gun towards me. Lightening brightens the sky as he stated with so much animosity, "I loved every minute of the things I did to you. I got my enjoyment of making you afraid of me. The beatings, the torture was awesome to me. I loved seeing you spineless and pathetic as I would shoot at you or make you terrified of me."

Thunder roared and I shuttered. My Love stated with too much joy, "Fear not, you will be up there soon enough."

He looked at me as I tried speaking to his heart, "But I loved you with all I had. There was nothing I wouldn't have done for you."

Marcus must have heard something for he tilted his head, and I took the opportunity to react. As he started back facing me, I picked up the shovel and hit him as hard as I could on side the head. He dropped the gun and appeared to be stunned as he went headfirst in the hole with me. With the moonlight on my side, I began attacking him violently like never before. I kicked and kicked until he did not move.

Hysterically I began feeling around in the puddle for the gun. I couldn't see because the flashlight was still on top of the ground. Being nervous, I could not find the gun, but I could hear Marcus moaning with pain. Soon as I placed my hands on the gun ,he rammed my body into the hard dark earth. I dropped the gun. He started attacking me, but I could not let him win. Using anger as my fuel I ignited it with hatred for the man I loved by throwing muddy water into his face.

"You bitch!" he screamed as he tried to find me.

The Lord showed favor to me as I saw the shovel and so did he. I dashed to it, but he picked up the gun and shot in the air. I froze. He walked over to me and used his right hand to snatch me to him. Once he did that, he tightly secured my head in the pit of his elbow; I could not move. Marcus, with the gun in his left hand placed the barrel to my temple. I began to cry.

"It's too late to cry now!" He shouted in my ear.

As if we were in the spotlight, the flashlight beamed down on us. Marcus froze as we both heard, "Drop your gun daddy."

It was Elisabeth's voice. I never thought I would be so happy to hear a child of his in my life, but I am. A voice then asked, "You alright?"

It was Mr. Goss. I began to whimper and whimper. Marcus's hand was slightly on my mouth; therefore, I began yelling, "Help me! Help me! Please Elisabeth help me."

He tightens his hand upon my mouth and screamed as he jerked my head harder, "Shut up! My child won't help you. She loves me, not you!"

He did not take his eyes off me as he yelled back to his daughter, "Baby girl stay out of my business. This does not concern you. Go back home and take that boy toy with you."

Elisabeth screamed with tears, "Daddy this is my business! I brought Trey out here to show him how the land looks this time of night."

"Now that you've showed him, you both can leave. I have some unfinished business to do."

"I can't do that, daddy."

Marcus didn't say a word. Elisabeth spoke with a shaky voice, "Please drop the gun before I shoot. I don't want to shoot you."

"Are you going to let her get away with what she did to your old man?"

"Daddy, I heard you admitting to toying with her. I am ashamed of you!"

Marcus said louder and with temper, "Leave us alone! You never cared for her. Don't care now!"

"I care to do what is right and this is not right. I will not let you intentionally hurt her anymore."

Marcus was quiet. Mr. Goss threw me a rope as he said, "The police is on their way, Mr. Grady. Let Sarah go."

My husband still would not let me go. Elisabeth began crying as she spoke louder with fear, "Daddy please don't make me do it!"

"You won't shoot your old man, Elisabeth. I am your father."

He must have felt that his daughter was not going to give in. Marcus loosens his grip on my mouth as he kissed me on the side of my face and smelled my hair. He whispered, "No one will ever love you like I do."

He made a motion to pull the trigger as Elisabeth shot him dead.

Epilogue

Sarah went back to school and became a psychologist for the emotionally disturbed and she never remarried.

Elisabeth and Mr. Goss finally got married and she did no time in jail because it was a life-or-death situation.

www.ingramcontent.com/pod-product-compliance
Lightning Source LLC
Chambersburg PA
CBHW021507240626
47154CB00002B/533